Title | The Sound of Madness
Author | Emmanuele Landini

CW01084630

Emmanuele Landini

THE SOUND OF MADNESS

(Remember to breathe, you cannot escape)

Preface:

There is a thin veil that separates reality from madness, life from death. In this labyrinth of shadows, where fear is the only companion, the protagonists of this story will find themselves confronting the unknown. In a world where survival is the only law, the characters of this tale will have to make difficult choices and face their greatest fears. An exhilarating journey through the depths of the human soul. Hidden truths and a past that returns to knock at the door will drag them into a vortex of unexpected events.

As you delve into this intricate plot, a constant sound—a faint ticking or an unsettling whisper—will accompany you, wearing down your nerves and pushing you towards madness. The pages of this book are a labyrinth of enigmas and tension where every turn hides a new danger.

This novel, incisive and at the same time thrilling, offers a realistic portrayal of individuals grappling with their greatest fears and weaves an intricate plot of insane events. Nothing is as it seems; shadows lengthen over a world where orientation and disorientation intertwine in a tense atmosphere that will keep you on the edge of your seat until the last word. Prepare yourself to uncover buried secrets and to unravel mysteries that will test your certainties.

Don't be fooled by appearances; nothing is as it seems in this thriller that will force you to reassess every certainty.

Introduction:

Every mile that separated her from Richmond seemed to stretch endlessly, as if the road bent under the weight of the past pulling her back. Bet Swanson gripped the steering wheel of her old Ford, trying in vain to keep at bay the thoughts that inevitably surfaced as she drew closer to the city. The hot air, thick with dust and the scent of dry earth, flowed in through the rolled-down windows, gently brushing against her copper-colored hair, tousled and rebellious as always. Every bend, every familiar glimpse of the countryside from her past, brought her closer to a world she had desperately tried to leave behind.

Richmond, the city where she had grown up, was a painful memory, but not just because of its stifling size or lack of opportunity. It was her father's premature death that had truly broken her, making her realize she could never stay there. He had passed away suddenly, just months before Bet graduated, leaving her alone with a mother who couldn't understand her. He had been the only real connection Bet had felt to that home, the only person who, in some way, understood her world of art, dreams, and colors. When he died, any hope of finding a semblance of peace in that city died with him.

The anger and grief from that loss had transformed into a fierce determination: she had to leave, she had to find something bigger. That determination had pushed her to board that train to New York, to leave Richmond, her mother, and everything she knew behind, in pursuit of a life she thought was meant for her.

Now, however, that life didn't seem as clear anymore. The chaotic streets of New York had promised success and fulfillment, but had instead drawn her into a daily struggle for survival. Her degrees in philosophy and art, which were supposed to open important doors, had left her with little more than a ticket to a competitive and ruthless jungle. She had always dreamed of opening an art gallery, of creating a space where artists could express themselves freely, where she, with her keen eye and sensitivity, could shape a unique artistic world. But New York hadn't been generous. Bet found herself doing odd jobs, serving coffee, selling paintings she didn't love, all in an effort to pay the rent on an apartment too small to hold her dreams.

The city's skyline began to emerge on the horizon, bathed in an orange sunset that turned the fields into golden waves. Richmond hadn't changed, or at least it seemed that way from a distance. But inside her, everything was different. She had left with the desire to conquer the world, to prove to her mother – and perhaps to herself – that she didn't need anyone, that she could achieve her dreams without being chained by the narrow expectations of a small provincial town.

Her mother. Bet couldn't recall the last time they had really spoken, aside from brief phone conversations, filled with awkward silences and obligatory phrases. When she left, they had fought furiously. Margaret Swanson had never approved of her decision to leave, seeing it as an irresponsible escape, a rejection of the stability Richmond could have offered her. Her father's death had only intensified the tension between them. Margaret, in her grief, had closed herself off even more, becoming cold and distant, unable to offer Bet the comfort she had so desperately needed.

And now Bet was coming back. Not by choice, but out of necessity. The call from the nurse had shattered the fragile balance she had maintained for years: "Your mother isn't well," the voice had said, in a tone that brooked no argument. There had been no choice. Even though Bet had tried to ignore that call, knowing what returning would mean, in the end she had to give in. Perhaps the time that had passed would allow them to rebuild that broken bond. Perhaps, but she didn't really believe it.

As the car rolled down the city's main road, childhood memories resurfaced with painful clarity. Days spent playing in the fields behind the house, the sweet scent of hay and damp earth, the heat of the sun burning her skin during the endless southern summers. Bet remembered running along those same roads with her father, her hands clasped in his, listening to the stories he made up to make her laugh. He had been the only one who understood that artistic side of Bet, her desire to express herself through painting, her sensitivity in seeing the world differently from others. Her mother, on the other hand, had never understood that passion. She had always been too focused on practical things, on the duties of everyday life.

The rusty sign marking the entrance to Richmond appeared before her, and Bet felt her stomach tighten. Her mother's old white house, nestled among the trees, was just minutes away. The years spent away from that place seemed to vanish, along with the fragile independence she had tried to build. She was no longer the dream-filled girl who had left Richmond. She had grown, she had fought, but deep down she still felt lost. She had abandoned that town hoping to find her path, but instead, she had found herself wandering, without a true purpose.

The driveway to the house opened up in front of her, and Bet turned off the engine. She sat for a moment, her hands trembling slightly on the wheel. Silence enveloped her, and the memory of her father hit her like a sudden pang. His absence was still a deep void, a void she had never been able to fill, neither in New York nor anywhere else.

She took a deep breath, closing her eyes for a moment. Returning had never been part of the plan, but now she had no choice. She had to face everything she had left behind, including the pain, including the memories that still haunted her.

With one final breath, she opened the car door. It was time to go home.

Chapter 1: Return to Richmond

Bet Swanson gripped the steering wheel of her old Ford tightly, a wreck held together more by providence than mechanics. Every mile she drove toward Richmond seemed to add a new creak, another ominous sound. The summer heat was unbearable; the air conditioning hadn't worked in years, and the open window let in nothing but hot air and dust.

The roads leading to Richmond were familiar, but something was different this time. Maybe it was just the marks of time, or perhaps the weight of the years spent away, but Bet couldn't shake a slight sense of unease. The trees lining the road seemed darker, their shadows longer and more menacing, like arms reaching out toward her. There was no concrete reason for her discomfort, but every turn, every mile, brought her closer to a growing sense of oppression deep inside. She tried to convince herself it was just fatigue or guilt, or perhaps a trick of the mind that had been away from these places for too long.

Finally, her mother's old house appeared on the horizon, a familiar dot in a world that now seemed more foreign than she remembered. The house was a wooden structure, its paint once white but now grayish with age, with shutters that creaked slightly in the wind. Margaret Swanson stood on the porch, one hand raised in greeting, the other resting on her frail hip, her face marked by the years but lit by a smile that brought a bit of warmth to Bet's heart. Her once golden hair was now faded and tied back with one of the pearl pins she so loved.

Margaret's eyes, dulled by time and illness, studied Bet, trying to recognize the almost forgotten features, but with a joy in her heart only a mother knows. She had never been a woman of many words, and her silences were often sharp, but time seemed to have softened her expression.

"You've finally arrived," Margaret said, her voice a little hoarse but still sweet.

When Bet got out of the car, her mother pulled her into a tight embrace, and for a moment, everything felt right. "Did you have a good trip?"

"Long and hot," Bet replied, trying not to show the discomfort she carried inside. "But I'm here, and that's all that matters."

Margaret nodded, observing her daughter with sharp eyes. "You're thinner than I remember, and those eyes… they carry more shadows than when you left."

Bet shrugged. "It's been tough years, but I'm fine. And how are you, Mom? Ever since I heard about your health, I haven't been able to stop thinking about how long it's been since I last called. I'm sorry. The house looks just as I left it…"

"This old place holds up," Margaret replied with a tired smile. "A bit like me, I suppose. Come inside, I made some fresh lemonade. In this heat, it's the only thing that'll give you some relief."

They went inside, where the air was cooler. The living room was exactly as Bet remembered: old furniture, a vintage radio in the corner, and wooden floors that creaked underfoot. Everything spoke of a bygone era, of a life Bet had tried to leave behind, but now enveloped her once again, like a heavy, suffocating blanket.

Margaret moved toward the kitchen and poured lemonade into two tall glasses, handing one to Bet. "Sit down, dear. Tell me something, it's been so long."

Bet's mother had been struck by a bone disease that slowly caused her body to stiffen more and more. Bet felt guilty for leaving her alone all these years, but she didn't know how to tell her. The two had never had deep conversations; it was always her father who had been her anchor.

Bet sat at the kitchen table, her gaze wandering over the details she had memorized during her childhood: the faded tablecloth, the thin cracks in the wooden table, the ticking of the wall clock marking each second with a slow, steady rhythm.

She took a sip of the lemonade, tasting the sweet and sour flavor melting on her tongue, bringing back memories of distant summers when everything seemed simpler.

"You know," Bet began, "I've always thought Richmond was a place without possibilities, static and old, but somehow, I've always felt it was safe, a refuge from the world. But now that I'm back, it feels different. It's like... like something has changed, but I don't know what."

Margaret watched her closely, then got up to look out the window, the curtains barely moving. "Everything changes, Bet. Even places we think have stayed the same. Sometimes it's our perception that shifts, other times it's the places themselves. Richmond has seen a lot over the years, but it's still our home. Even if..." She let the sentence hang in the air, as if there was something left unsaid, something she didn't want to face.

"Even if what?" Bet asked, but Margaret shook her head.

"Nothing, just the thoughts of an old woman. Come, let me show you the garden. I've tried to keep it the way you liked it, but this year's heat has taken a toll on the plants."

They went outside to the backyard, where the once-lush garden showed signs of wear. The plants Bet remembered as tall and vibrant were now tired and drooping, like soldiers defeated in a battle against the relentless sun. The roses, which Margaret had always tended with so much love, had withered, their dry petals scattered on the ground like forgotten tears.

"Mom, you did your best. But this heat... I don't know how you manage."

Margaret shrugged. "You get used to it, I suppose. And besides, this garden has survived worse summers. With a bit of luck, it'll survive this one too." Her face, worn by time, carried a faint smile.

Bet couldn't help but feel there was something deeply sad in those words, a sense of resignation she hadn't heard before.

She looked at the garden again, trying to find the beauty she once saw there, but her eyes fell instead on an old stone well, hidden in a corner, almost swallowed by the shadows. She remembered playing there as a child, throwing pebbles into the deep darkness, imagining what might be down there, hidden beneath the surface.

"Do you remember when I used to play near that well?" she asked, pointing to the old structure. "You once told me never to look into it for too long, that I'd see something I wouldn't want to see." Bet felt a chill run down her spine.

Margaret turned slowly, her eyes now filled with an expression Bet couldn't decipher. "Some things are better left alone, Bet. Some questions shouldn't be asked, and some answers... shouldn't be found."

Bet recalled how cryptic her mother could be, but decided to let it go, not wanting to relive the past.

They spent the afternoon talking about the days when Bet was a child and Richmond seemed like an entire world, full of secrets to discover and adventures to live. Margaret recounted stories of when Bet was little, running through the trees behind the house, coming back with scraped knees and dirt-stained clothes but a smile that lit up the world. Bet felt safe in those memories, where every run, every adventure, every game with her childhood friend was lived with lightness, free from the heavy thoughts of later years.

As they talked, Bet's eyes fell on an old framed photograph displayed on a cabinet in the living room. The dark wooden frame was carefully carved, and the image showed a young man with dark hair and a sincere smile: her father. Memories flooded her mind, and for a moment, she felt an emptiness in her chest, as if time had rewound, and the pain of his loss returned to the surface.

Bet stood and picked up the photo, studying the face of the man who had meant so much to her. "Dad..." she murmured, almost without realizing it.

Margaret watched her in silence, her hands clasped in her lap. "You look like him, you know? You have his same look: strong, but with a hidden softness not everyone can see."

Bet nodded, without taking her eyes off the picture. "I miss him. Sometimes I wonder what he would've said if he were here today. Would he have told me I made the right choices?"

Margaret got up and approached Bet, gently placing a hand on her shoulder. "Your father was a wise man. He would have understood your choices, even if he didn't agree with all of them. And he would have always found a way to make you feel loved. You were his little girl."

Bet felt the tears well up, but she held them back. "I remember when he used to take me to the lake in the summer. We'd spend hours fishing, and he'd tell me scary stories to keep me awake. But they were never too scary because he knew I was afraid of the dark," she said, breathing deeply.

Margaret smiled wistfully. "He had a gift for finding that delicate balance between the real and the imaginary. And, in a way, he was a bit like Richmond. He knew how to keep secrets, but he also knew when to share them."

"Not only that," Bet replied, "He always understood what I carried inside, always pushed me not to give up and to believe in myself. When he passed, I felt completely lost," she said in a trembling voice, as her eyes fought to hold back the tears. "Believe me, Mom, I'm sorry I left you here alone. Now, after all these years, I realize it wasn't easy for you either, but this place brought me too much pain. I couldn't stay

Margaret took a few steps back, lowering her gaze. "I loved your father very much, but life was hard for us, and I don't blame you for your choices," she replied softly, though there was a faint edge to her tone, as if holding back her own pain. "Richmond is my home. It's always been, and it will be yours too, whenever you want. Even if..." She trailed off, her eyes flicking to the photograph of Bet's father. "Even if I know I've never been to

you what he was."

Bet gently placed the photo back, her hands moving with delicate precision, almost as if afraid of disturbing the stillness of the memory. "Sometimes it feels like I can still hear his voice, you know? Like he's still here, somewhere."

Margaret didn't respond, but the silence that followed was thick with meaning. It was a tacit understanding between mother and daughter, an unspoken agreement not to let the past consume them.

As evening fell, bringing with it some relief from the suffocating heat, Bet felt a wave of exhaustion wash over her. The clothes she had worn during the long drive were crumpled, soaked with sweat, and her tousled hair begged for a refreshing rinse.

The journey, the return home, the memories resurfacing like bubbles in murky water—all of it was taking its toll.

"I'm going to take a shower and head to bed, Mom. Tomorrow, I want to go into town, see some of the old places again."

Margaret nodded. "That's fine, dear. Your old room is ready, just as you left it. The shower sometimes spits out water here and there, but otherwise, it works. I should get it fixed."

Bet bid her mother goodnight and retreated to her room—a small oasis of the past, where everything seemed frozen in time. The walls were still adorned with posters of bands she had loved as a teenager, and the bed was covered with the same floral blanket she had always hated, though now it gave her a strange sense of comfort. "A cool shower is just what I need," she thought, slipping under the uneven flow of the water.

Once out of the shower, Bet looked at herself in the mirror, feeling tired and worn. She ran her hands over her face, searching for wrinkles that weren't there yet.

She had never particularly liked the way she looked, but over time, she had learned to accept the image she saw in the mirror—her porcelain skin, tinged with rosy cheeks, and her slightly full lips, always carrying a subtle expression of melancholy. Her deep blue eyes, marked by the strain of the journey, craved a long, restorative sleep.

She pulled her copper hair up into a messy bun with a large hair tie and changed into an old set of pajamas she had left behind years ago, slipping under the covers.

She closed her eyes, trying to surrender to sleep, but something kept her awake. A distant sound, barely audible but constant. She tossed and turned in bed, but the sound persisted, a faint chirring that seemed to come from everywhere—from beneath the windows, from the walls themselves.

"Bet, it's just the cicadas," she told herself. "The soundtrack of Richmond's summer nights." Nothing to worry about. She was tired, and the long trip had worn her out. But as she tried to close her eyes once more, she couldn't help but feel that the sound, once so familiar and comforting, now carried something unsettling, something different.

Bet forced herself not to dwell on it, finally letting sleep take her, with the promise that she would explore the town the next day. But deep in her heart, something gnawed at her—a feeling she couldn't shake, as if Richmond were whispering in her ear, trying to tell her something she didn't want to hear.

Chapter 2: The Sleeping City

Bet woke up the next morning with a slight headache, perhaps due to the restless sleep she had experienced the night before. The sound of cicadas, which she had heard late into the night, still seemed to ring in her ears, but she attributed the sensation to accumulated fatigue. After all, she had traveled for hours to reach Richmond, and coming back home, with all the emotional baggage it carried, had not been easy.

She yawned and stretched in bed, feeling her stiff muscles relax slightly. Her old room was bathed in a golden light, with the sun's rays filtering through the light curtains. It was a small refuge of peace, where time seemed to have stood still, but Bet knew she couldn't stay there forever. Today, she would take a walk around town to see how much Richmond had changed during her absence.

She took a light dress from her suitcase, and after getting dressed, she went downstairs and found her mother in the kitchen, preparing breakfast. The smell of freshly brewed coffee filled the air, mixing with the aroma of toasted bread.

"Good morning," Bet said, trying to mask the tiredness in her voice.

Margaret turned and smiled at her. "Good morning, dear. Did you sleep well?"

"Well enough," Bet replied, grabbing a cup and pouring herself some coffee, trying to shake off the strange feeling she had and the memories that often resurfaced in her mind. "It seems like the cicadas were noisier than usual."

Margaret nodded slowly, looking out the window. "They've been particularly persistent this year, don't you think? It's strange, but I suppose it's normal with this heat."

Bet didn't reply, sipping her coffee as her thoughts wandered. There was something unspoken in her mother's words, something Bet couldn't quite decipher, but she decided not to press the issue. It was her first day in Richmond, and she wanted to live it without too many dark thoughts, doing her best to support her mother.

"I was thinking of taking a walk around town today," Bet said, trying to change the subject. "Revisit some places, maybe catch up with a few old friends."

Margaret looked at her with a warm smile, but her gaze drifted for a moment, as if lost in thought. "That's a good idea," she said, placing a plate of scrambled eggs and bacon in front of her. "Richmond may seem the same as always, but sometimes things change without us even noticing." She paused, as if considering whether to say more, then concluded in a slightly lighter tone, "But you know this town better than anyone."

Bet hoped that was true, but she knew time had a strange way of changing things, even those that seemed unchanging. After finishing breakfast, she left the house.

She looked around; the air felt thin, and the sweltering heat was relentless even in the early morning. The sky was clear, and the driveway was lined with plants struggling to stay green. She took a deep breath—taking the car would only make things worse—so she decided to walk into Richmond.

As she walked through the city streets, Bet noticed that the cicadas' chirping seemed louder than the day before. It was a sound that insinuated itself between the walls of the houses, bounced off the asphalt of the empty streets, and echoed in every corner. It almost felt like the city itself was vibrating to the rhythm of that incessant chirping. Bet stopped for a moment, trying to figure out if it was just her imagination, but the sound was there, constant and strangely oppressive.

The streets were surprisingly empty for a mid-week morning. Stores were slowly opening, their signs creaking slightly under the hot wind. Bet walked at a slow pace, observing every detail closely. Richmond was exactly as she remembered it: the same central square with the fountain in the middle, the same old houses facing cobbled streets. And yet, something felt different, something subtly unsettling that Bet couldn't quite define.

As she crossed the square, she noticed a group of people walking on the opposite side of the street.

There was something odd about their steps, as if they were trying to synchronize with each other, but in an unnatural, forced way. A woman caught Bet's gaze, and for a moment, Bet felt a shiver run down her spine: the woman's eyes were empty, devoid of any expression, as if she were looking right through her.

She shook her head, trying to dismiss the thought. Maybe it was just her imagination playing tricks on her.

She decided to step into the old café on the corner, a place she often frequented during her teenage years. She paused for a moment to look at the entrance, the green door, and the semi-broken sign that had never been repaired, reading *Mokka*. When she crossed the threshold, the tinkling of the bell above the door immediately brought back memories of afternoons spent there, sitting at one of the tables, sipping lemonade and reading books.

Inside, the atmosphere was almost surreal. The dim light filtering through the windows cast long, distorted shadows on the walls. Only a couple of customers sat at the tables, speaking in hushed tones. The barista, a middle-aged woman with brown hair tied in a tight bun, stood behind the counter, slowly drying a cup with a cloth.

Bet approached the counter, trying to shake off the strange sense of unease that was creeping over her. "A coffee, please," she said, trying to smile.

The barista looked up and gave her a smile that seemed more like a grimace. "Sure, right away," she replied in a nearly mechanical tone. As she prepared the coffee, Bet noticed that her movements were slow, deliberate, as if she were doing everything automatically.

Bet glanced around, noting that the few customers present all had the same absent expression. They spoke to each other, but there was no real conversation, just a monotone murmur that blended with the distant sound of the cicadas' chirping. One of the men at the table stared at her without blinking, as if trying to decipher something hidden within her.

The barista set the coffee cup down on the counter in front of Bet. "Pay now or later?" she asked in a tone that left no room for variation.

"Now is fine," Bet replied, trying to hide the growing discomfort inside her. She pulled out her straw-colored wallet from her leather backpack, and as she paid, the barista looked her straight in the eyes. For a moment, Bet thought she saw something unsettling behind that gaze, like a shadow moving just beneath the surface, but she couldn't quite make it out.

"Thank you," the barista said, but her tone was devoid of warmth, almost as if she were reciting a line she had repeated too many times.

Bet took her cup and sat at a table near the window. The wooden chair creaked, but it seemed sturdy enough to support her without issue. She sipped the coffee, but the taste was bitter, different from what she remembered. Maybe it was just the passage of time, or maybe something had truly changed in this town. As she gazed out the foggy window, she saw a man walk by, his eyes fixed ahead. He walked with a stiff, almost robotic gait. Bet wondered if everyone in town had transformed like this, if the Richmond she remembered existed only in her memories.

After finishing her coffee, Bet decided to continue her walk. She left the café with a sense of relief, as if she had just left a place that was trying to swallow her whole. The streets were still strangely empty, and the few people she passed all had that same odd air, that mechanical and unnatural behavior that had disturbed her in the café.

As she walked, she approached the old record store, and a strange feeling washed over her. It had been one of her favorite places as a teenager; she would spend hours there searching for records by her favorite bands. However, the shop was closed, its windows coated in dust and the lights off. A faded sign announced that the owner had moved elsewhere, and Bet couldn't help but feel a pang of sadness. That shop had been a refuge for her and her childhood friend, a place where they could lose themselves in music and forget the outside world during those afternoons spent listening to records.

She was about to turn and leave when, almost without thinking, she placed her hand on the door handle. She expected it to be locked, but to her surprise, the handle gave way easily under her grip. The door creaked open, revealing the dark, dusty interior of the shop. She hesitated for a moment, then decided to enter.

Inside, the air was stale and thick with dust. Light barely filtered through the dirty windows, creating an otherworldly atmosphere, almost suspended in time. The shelves, once filled with records, were now nearly empty, save for a few old records scattered here and there like debris left behind by a receding tide.

Bet walked slowly between the deserted rows, looking at the dust-covered covers of the few remaining records. There was something profoundly sad about the place, as if time had swallowed every trace of life. Yet Bet couldn't shake the feeling that there was something strange beneath the desolation. A strong sense of unease washed over her as she continued to explore the shop.

She stopped in front of a particularly dilapidated shelf, where one record caught her attention. It was almost buried under a layer of dust, and the cover was so faded that the colors were barely distinguishable. With a decisive gesture, Bet

picked it up and blew off the dust, revealing the title etched in vibrant but now worn letters: *The Sound of the Cicadas*.

Bet frowned, staring in disbelief at the title. It was too strange a coincidence, considering how much that sound had dominated her thoughts in the past twenty-four hours. The cover of the record was equally unsettling: it depicted a desolate rural landscape, with a barren tree in the foreground and, in the distance, a ruined house. The cicadas, drawn in an almost grotesque style, were scattered throughout the scene, depicted with such attention to detail that they appeared incredibly alive, almost pulsing.

She turned the record over, examining the back of the cover. The back depicted a wooded environment, with dense trees and shadows stretching in all directions. At the center of the image was some sort of cave, a dark opening between the rocks, partially hidden among the vegetation. The cicadas seemed to be gathered around the entrance to the cave, as if they were drawn to something inside, something invisible but irresistible. The image was disturbing, and Bet couldn't tell if it was just her imagination or if there was truly something sinister about the scene.

The record itself looked old but not too worn. There were no notes on the back about the year of release or the artist. It seemed like a forgotten product, but somehow preserved intact in that place. Bet felt a chill run down her spine as she examined the record. Something about this was wrong, but she couldn't tear her eyes away from the cover.

She decided to take it with her. Even though logic told her to leave it there, something urged her to find out more. "I'll ask my mother," she thought, "maybe she knows something about this record and the shop."

With the record in hand, Bet headed for the exit. As she turned to leave, she thought she heard a faint sound, different from the cicadas' chirping. It was like a whisper, a distant murmur coming from somewhere in the shadows. She stopped, trying to figure out where the sound was coming from, but all she could hear was the rapid beating of her heart.

Bet left the shop with an unsettling feeling she couldn't explain, the record clutched in her hands like a piece of a puzzle she didn't yet know how to put together. Richmond was beginning to reveal its secrets, and Bet felt that this was only the beginning.

Chapter 3: The Call of the Past

The next morning arrived with a lazy sun rising behind the horizon, casting Richmond in a golden light, deceptively peaceful. Bet woke up with a feeling of unease, her head heavy and her body wrapped in a lethargy she couldn't shake off. The chirping of the cicadas, which had even invaded her dreams, continued incessantly outside the window, like a thin, persistent thread tying reality to the dream world.

Despite it being only morning, the air was already hot, thick with humidity, and it seemed to cling to her skin. The oppressive heat of that summer had become a constant presence, like an invisible figure that followed Bet everywhere she went, amplifying her sense of discomfort and uncertainty.

She pulled on a pair of shorts and went downstairs, finding her mother already busy with breakfast.

The familiar smell of coffee and toast surrounded her, but there was something different in the air, a subtle tension she couldn't quite define. Margaret, moving with an unusual nervousness, merely smiled at her when Bet greeted her with a good morning, but the smile never reached her eyes.

Bet sat at the table, staring at the plate of scrambled eggs before her. She had lost her appetite, but forced herself to eat, as if keeping up a ritual that tied her to a distant sense of normalcy. Every bite was tasteless, as if the food were merely a formality, an empty gesture. The coffee sank heavy in her stomach like a stone. The oppressive heat seemed to amplify every sensation, making everything feel more intense and unbearable.

Bet couldn't shake the sense of unease, worsened by the heat that seemed to amplify every negative emotion. The thought of the record she had found the day before plagued her. So, after breakfast, she decided to take a closer look. She returned to her room, took the record out of her bag, and placed it on the bed. The faded cover and the disturbing image on the back seemed to radiate negative energy, a weight that grew heavier with each passing moment.

She set up her old record player and placed the record on the turntable. When she lowered the needle, there was a moment of silence, followed by the soft crackle of the vinyl, which Bet found strangely comforting. But as soon as the sound of cicadas started to emerge from the speakers, that feeling quickly turned into a creeping anxiety. The sound was identical to what she had heard all night, but there was something more—an eerie tone that seemed to burrow under her skin, growing a sense of discomfort inside her.

The chirping became more intense, enveloping the room in a suffocating atmosphere. Bet closed her eyes, trying to concentrate, but the sound disoriented her, making her lose track of time. It was as if the cicadas' noise were pulling her into a spiral of confusion and fear.

Suddenly, the door to her room flew open with a loud bang. Margaret rushed in, her face pale and her eyes wide with terror. Without a word, she hurried to the record player and, with an abrupt gesture, lifted the needle, cutting the sound short. Then, without hesitation, she grabbed the record and its cover, holding them tightly in her trembling hand.

"Mom!" Bet exclaimed, startled by her mother's sudden reaction. "What are you doing?"

Margaret didn't respond immediately. Clutching the record to her chest, she looked at Bet with a gaze full of concern. "Did you listen to the whole thing?" she asked, her voice trembling slightly.

"No, just part of it... why?" Bet looked at her mother, confused, her heart pounding.

Margaret closed her eyes for a moment as if trying to calm herself, then reopened them, fixing Bet with an intense stare. "This record... must not be listened to. You don't understand what it could do."

"But what's so dangerous about an old record?" Bet asked, trying to comprehend her mother's distress.

Margaret shook her head, her eyes still locked on Bet's. "Some things, Bet, must stay in the past. They're not meant to be listened to... or understood. I can't explain everything, but you have to trust me. Stay away from this record."

Bet felt a chill run down her spine. "But... why? Why can't I listen to it? What are you hiding from me?"

Margaret buried her face in her hands, as if battling thoughts she didn't want to share. "It's not the record, Bet... it's what it might awaken."

Bet's heart raced, but her mother refused to say more. "What am I supposed to do?"

Margaret looked at her, her eyes filled with a desperation Bet had never seen before. "Don't ever listen to it again. Promise me you won't try to understand more. Some secrets are too dangerous."

Bet nodded slowly, her heart filled with fear and confusion. She couldn't fully grasp the weight of what her mother was saying, but she knew the terror in her eyes was real. Margaret turned and, with the record still clutched to her chest, left the room without another word.

Bet remained motionless for a moment, trying to process what had just happened. Then, a sudden thought hit her: where was her mother going to take the record? And why did she seem so terrified? Curiosity, mixed with a sense of urgency, took over.

Silently, Bet got up and followed her mother stealthily down the stairs. Margaret moved with unusual haste, as if she wanted to get rid of the record as quickly as possible. Bet, her heart pounding, followed at a distance, careful not to be noticed.

Margaret left the house and headed toward the old tool shed at the far end of the garden. It was a place Bet barely remembered, a disused building with a creaky door and windows covered in dust. The heat outside was even more oppressive, and the deafening noise of the cicadas made every step feel more laborious. Margaret opened the door to the shed and disappeared inside. Bet crept closer, hiding behind a large tree, watching through a crack in the half-open door.

She saw her mother open an old wooden chest, the kind used to store valuable or dangerous items. Margaret placed the record inside with extreme care, almost reverently, as if handling a sacred or cursed object. Then, she closed the chest, turned an old rusty lock, and hid the key under a stone beside the chest.

Bet held her breath as Margaret left the shed, closing the door behind her. She waited for her mother to be far enough away, then stealthily approached the shed. Her heart raced as she opened the creaky door and stepped into the darkness. The light barely filtered through the dusty windows, creating an oppressive atmosphere.

She approached the chest, the lock still fastened with the key hidden under the stone. The urge to open it was overwhelming, but at the same time, Bet felt a growing fear, a dread that stopped her from acting. After a long moment of hesitation, she decided to hurry. She grabbed the key and unlocked the chest, her forehead damp with sweat from the fear of being caught by her mother. She quickly closed the shed door and headed back toward the house, an eerie sense of unease following her like a shadow.

She rushed back to her room and hid the record in a large bag. Going downstairs, she saw Margaret outside in the garden through the large kitchen window. As she took a sip of coffee, Bet felt an inexplicable urge to leave the house. She decided she needed to talk to someone she trusted, someone who could help her make sense of what was happening. The image of James, her childhood friend, came to mind almost immediately. If anyone could understand the significance of that record, it was him.

She grabbed the bag with the vinyl, the keys to her old Ford, and left. The summer air hit her like a wall as soon as she stepped outside. The heat was almost unbearable, thick with humidity and dust, and every step toward the car felt more difficult than the last. She got into the car and started the engine, which sputtered for a moment before roaring to life. She rolled down the windows in a futile attempt to let in some fresh air, but all she got was a hot breeze hitting her face.

As she drove through the streets of Richmond, her thoughts began to drift back in time. Every corner of the town seemed to hold a memory. There was the old cinema where she and James used to watch horror movies on Saturday nights, laughing and joking to hide how scared they really were. She remembered the bike rides along the dirt roads, with the wind tangling her hair and James's laughter filling the air. He had always been like that: a free spirit, a gentle rebel who lived for music and dreamed of becoming a great musician, even though life seemed to thwart his every attempt.

Bet had never told anyone, but as a girl, she had secretly been in love with James. She admired him from afar, keeping those feelings to herself, feelings that filled her heart every time she watched him play guitar, his fingers moving gracefully across the strings as if it came naturally to him. She had always found the courage to be his friend, but never anything more. There were times she wondered if James had ever noticed something in her eyes, a spark of the love she tried to hide.

Even now, as she drove toward him, Bet felt her heart beat a little faster. Years had passed, things had changed, she had changed and had had to leave, but those feelings had never completely faded, and her heart knew it. She wondered what he was like now, what was left of the boy she had once known. She had often imagined what it would be like to see him again, whether the passing of time had altered their bond or if it would feel as though not a single day had passed.

After a few more miles, she reached James's house, an old colonial home standing at the end of a dirt road. The garden was overgrown, with tall, yellowed grass scorched by the relentless sun, and the plants seemed to have succumbed to the oppressive heat. Bet turned off the engine and got out of the car, feeling the dry, dusty ground crackle under her feet. The heat was suffocating, and the air was thick with the dry scent of earth.

She stood in front of the door for a moment, unsure of what to expect. She hadn't seen James in years, and her memories of him were tied to the carefree days of childhood, when Richmond was just a quiet little town, and the world seemed free of shadows. Bet gathered her courage and knocked, the sound echoing through the thick, cicada-filled air.

There was a brief silence, followed by the sound of slow footsteps approaching from inside. The door creaked open, and James appeared on the threshold. He looked tired, with an unkempt beard and messy hair, but when his eyes met Bet's, a surprised smile spread across his face.

"Bet!" he exclaimed with genuine enthusiasm, his wide brown eyes lighting up. Without a second thought, he grabbed her by the shoulders and pulled her into a warm hug, as if no time had passed at all.

Bet stood frozen for a moment, enveloped in his strong embrace, surprised by the familiarity of the gesture, then she allowed herself to relax, feeling the warmth of his body against hers. A strange excitement surged through her chest, a mix of nostalgia and something deeper, something she thought she had buried years ago. Perhaps those feelings she had as a young girl were still there, hidden beneath the surface, ready to resurface.

"It's been so long," Bet murmured, trying to steady her voice as she pulled back slightly, but without breaking eye contact for even a moment.

James looked at her with a smile that seemed to say more than words ever could. "Too long," he replied, his voice full of sweetness. "How are you? Where have you been? How's life treating you?"

Bet smiled, a mix of shyness and sincerity. "I'm getting by," she said, trying to keep the tone light. "After college, I worked here and there in New York, trying to find my way. I stayed in the city for a while, but now I'm back in Richmond to take care of my mom."

James nodded, listening intently, as if every word she said mattered. "I'm glad you're back," he said with genuine warmth. "Life here hasn't changed much, but I imagine you've had your fair share of new experiences."

"Yeah," Bet replied, twirling a strand of her hair like she used to when she was nervous as a teenager. "But it's strange how the things you leave behind have a way of coming back. Richmond always had a kind of... magnetism, don't you think?"

"Absolutely," James said with a knowing smile, then invited her inside. "Come on in, there's something I want to show you."

As Bet stepped inside, she noticed the room was filled with musical instruments: a guitar propped up against a chair, an old piano in the corner, and even a bass guitar on a stand. But what truly caught her attention was the makeshift recording studio in an adjacent room, complete with microphones, headphones, and a computer loaded with recording software. It was clear that James had never given up on his musical dream.

"Wow, you've really got quite the setup here," Bet said, looking around with admiration.

"It's nothing special," James replied modestly, though Bet could see a flicker of pride in his eyes.

"But it keeps me busy. I've spent the last few years writing and recording music. It's not easy, but it's what I love to do."

"You've always been a musician at heart," Bet said, feeling a strange emotion rising inside her as she looked at James with a wistful expression. Her heart beat faster at the thought of how much she had always admired him and, perhaps, secretly loved him.

James gestured for her to sit in the living room, where the air was cooler thanks to an old fan buzzing lazily in the corner. Even though the room was dimly lit, Bet noticed that it was filled with records, old vinyl, and stacks of music magazines, as if time had frozen in those objects.

They sat on a faded light-gray couch, worn by time, and Bet pulled out the record she had taken from the shed before leaving the house. When she placed it on the coffee table, James looked at it with interest, but also with a hint of concern.

"Where did you find this?" he asked, surprised, examining the faded cover.

"At the old record store," Bet replied. "But there's something strange about it. When I listened to it... I don't know how to explain it, James, but there's something wrong with that sound."

James was silent for a moment, then nodded slowly. "I've heard of records like this... records that shouldn't exist. They're like signals, keys to something that's better left unopened."

A chill ran down Bet's spine. "My mom knew. When she saw it, she was terrified. She hid it... and told me never to listen to it again."

James pondered her words. "She might be right. Sometimes there are things better left undiscovered. But if you're here, it means you want to find out the truth, don't you?"

Bet nodded. "I can't help it, James. There's something about that record and Richmond that

won't leave me alone. The cicadas… the sound…
the record, it's all connected. I need to understand
what's happening."

James sighed, staring at the record with an
expression Bet couldn't quite decipher. "If that's
what you want… then we'll have to be very
careful. We might not like what we find."

The tension in the air seemed to rise with the heat
that continued to build, making the atmosphere
even more oppressive. Bet knew she had just taken
a step into unknown and dangerous territory, but
there was no turning back now. The shadows of the
past were beginning to surface, and she had no
choice but to face them.

Chapter 4: Into the Unknown

Bet and James decided not to waste any time. The oppressive heat of the day seemed to amplify the tension they both felt, a growing anxiety that drove them to uncover what was hidden behind the mysterious record. After discussing things further in the living room, James suggested they listen to the record together in his small recording studio, where they could analyze everything better without being disturbed.

"If there's something hidden in this music," James said, "we'll discover it here."

Bet hesitated for a moment, recalling her mother's words, but in the end, she agreed. She knew it was too late to turn back. She had to know what was happening, even if it meant facing something unknown and potentially dangerous.

James carefully picked up the record, as if he were afraid of breaking something fragile and precious. He placed it on the turntable in his studio, a small, intimate space filled with musical instruments, cables, and audio equipment. Bet noticed the professional way James handled everything, and for a brief moment, she felt reassured by his presence, as if time hadn't changed anything between them.

"Ready?" James asked, looking at her for a moment, perhaps searching for one last sign of hesitation.

Bet nodded, even though her heart was pounding. "Yes, go ahead."

James lowered the needle onto the record, and the soft crackle of the vinyl filled the room, followed by the sound of cicadas chirping—the same sound Bet had heard incessantly the night before and throughout the day in the streets of the city. But there was more: now, listening carefully in such an isolated environment, she could detect a sort of hidden melody, almost imperceptible but present. A melody that flowed and undulated, evoking images of dark forests and abandoned paths.

James listened in silence, his expression focused, but Bet could see a change in his eyes. There was something in that music that was touching deep chords within him, something that unsettled him. Bet felt increasingly uneasy as the sound continued to fill the room, wrapping around them like a shroud of darkness.

Suddenly, the cicadas' sound changed, becoming sharper, more piercing, like an alarm cry. James jolted and, with a swift movement, lifted the needle off the record, abruptly stopping the music. But instead of silence, a wave of darkness enveloped them. Both fainted simultaneously, without even realizing it.

The moment they lost consciousness, they found themselves immersed in a vivid and terrifying dream. Before them lay a dark forest, shrouded in a suffocating atmosphere. The chirping of cicadas was deafening, a continuous, penetrating sound that seemed to come from every direction. The trees were twisted, their shadows menacing, and the feeling of being watched grew stronger and stronger. At the far end of the forest, through the dark foliage, a cave appeared—a deep, black opening exuding a sense of impending danger and unease.

The cicadas, numerous and frantic, seemed to have gathered around the cave, as if drawn to it, called by something ancient and evil. The sound of their chirping intensified until it became nearly unbearable, a scream that pierced their ears and minds, forcing Bet and James to clutch their heads in a vain attempt to block it out.

When they awoke, dazed and confused, the vinyl was still spinning on the turntable, even though the needle was raised, hovering above it. For a few moments, they remained motionless, trying to recover, their hearts pounding and their breathing labored. Their faces were pale, almost ghostly, and the silence in the room was broken only by the hum of the fan and the faint rustling of the turntable.

"James..." Bet was the first to speak, her voice trembling. "Did you see it too... that forest? The cave? What was that?"

James nodded slowly, his eyes still filled with fear and confusion. "Yes... I saw it. It was so real, Bet. The sound of the cicadas... it was everywhere. And that cave..."

He trailed off, as if struggling to find the words to describe what he had seen. Then he abruptly turned toward the album cover lying on the table. Bet followed his gaze and felt a shiver run down her spine.

On the back cover of the record was an image they had both noticed but hadn't paid much attention to before: a dark forest with some kind of cave in the distance. It was exactly the scene they had just seen in their vision. The cicadas, seemingly pulsating in sync with the music, were depicted on the twisted branches of the trees, like a sinister omen.

"It's the same forest..." Bet whispered, almost in disbelief. "And the cave... it's the same one we saw."

James sank into a chair, running a trembling hand through his hair. "This record isn't just an object, Bet. There's something more... something that shouldn't exist. That vision... I don't know what it means, but it's tied to this record."

Bet tried to remain calm, but fear was growing inside her. "We need to figure out what's happening, James. But we have to be very careful. Whatever this is… it can't be good."

James nodded, still shaken. "I need to keep working on it. Maybe there's something we can do to better decipher what this record is showing us. But it's clear this isn't just music."

Bet looked again at the image on the cover, trying to understand how something so seemingly harmless could hide such a dark power. "It's like the record is a door," she said quietly, "and by listening to it, we've started to open it."

James looked at her, his face serious. "And we have to decide if we want to step through."

The silence that followed was heavy with tension, both of them aware of the danger they were facing. But they knew there was no turning back. They had to uncover the truth, even if it meant confronting the darkness they had glimpsed in their vision.

James stood up from the chair, seemingly calmer, though the pallor of his face betrayed the unease he still felt. "Bet," he said in a more measured tone, "leave the record with me. I want to work on it some more tomorrow morning, with a clearer head. Maybe I can find something to help us understand."

Bet hesitated for a moment, but she knew that James was the best person to handle the record. "Alright," she replied, handing him the object with slightly trembling hands. "But be careful, James. This isn't just any record."

James nodded, gripping the record firmly. "I know. Don't worry, Bet. I'll talk to you tomorrow."

Bet left James's house with a growing sense of unease, which seemed to intensify with every step toward her car. The evening heat was still oppressive, and the air felt charged with an indescribable tension. As she drove home, the chirping of the cicadas seemed to follow her, louder and more insistent than before.

When she arrived home, she immediately noticed something strange: the sound of the cicadas hadn't diminished with the onset of night, as it should have. Instead, it seemed louder than ever, a continuous chirping that filled the air with a disturbing energy. Bet got out of the car, her heart pounding, and walked toward the front door.

Entering the house, she found it in a state she hadn't expected. All the windows were open, and the sound of the cicadas filled every corner of the house, amplified and echoing through the walls. The lighting was dim, and the warm night air seemed to circulate freely, mixing with a sense of unease that made the atmosphere almost suffocating.

"Mom?" Bet called out, advancing cautiously. She found her mother in the living room, sitting in a chair, her gaze vacant. Margaret was in a catatonic state, her eyes glassy and her expression completely absent.

"Mom!" Bet repeated, this time more forcefully, shaking her mother slightly to get her to react. But Margaret didn't respond, as if she couldn't even hear her. Bet realized with horror that the cicadas' chirping seemed to be having a hypnotic effect on her, trapping her in that stupor.

Without wasting time, Bet began closing all the windows, one by one, trying to block out the deafening sound that seemed to penetrate every fiber of the house. Each window she closed seemed to slightly reduce the noise, but the sound was still too strong, too present to be completely ignored.

"Mom, wake up!" Bet said, this time with more urgency, as she shut the last window. She knelt beside Margaret, taking her cold hands in hers. "Please, Mom, wake up!"

After what felt like an eternity, Margaret finally blinked, as if waking from a long sleep. She looked around, confused, and then fixed her gaze on Bet with a mixture of terror and bewilderment.

"Bet?" she asked in a weak voice, as if unsure of where she was. "What... what happened?"

Bet hugged her tightly, relieved to see her finally respond. "I don't know, Mom. But you were... you were in a catatonic state, and the sound of the cicadas... it was everywhere."

Margaret brought a hand to her head, still visibly dazed. "I don't remember anything... the last thing

I recall is opening the windows to let some air in…
then… everything's blurry."

Bet helped her up from the chair and guided her to
her bedroom, where she had her lie down on the
bed. "Rest for a while, Mom," she said gently,
though inside, she was still shaken. "We'll talk
tomorrow."

Margaret weakly nodded, closing her eyes as Bet
covered her with a light blanket. Bet stayed by her
side for a moment, watching her breathe slowly,
until she fell into a deep sleep.

Bet stepped away from the room, feeling
exhausted and disturbed. As she closed her
mother's bedroom door, the sound of the cicadas
still echoed in her ears, an incessant chirping that
wouldn't stop. She sat down on the couch in the
living room, her mind a whirlwind of thoughts.

That night, despite her exhaustion, Bet couldn't
find peace. The sound of the cicadas, though
muffled by the closed windows, continued to echo
in her mind, mingling with the images from the
vision she had shared with James. It was clear that
the record had unleashed something—something

far beyond mere music. But what? And how could they stop it?

The next day would bring new answers, but Bet knew the road ahead was dangerous and full of unknowns. And as the night wore on, the cicadas' chirping continued, like a dark omen that refused to make way for silence.

Chapter 5: The Awakening of Madness

Bet woke up the next morning confused and worried about her mother, who, as usual, was busy in the kitchen preparing breakfast.

"Mom, how are you feeling?" Bet asked in a soft voice.

Margaret looked at her with sad eyes but said nothing, continuing to make toast and eggs as if doing the same thing every morning gave her a sense of normalcy.

"Would you like some coffee, dear?"

"Mom!" Bet said firmly, her worried gaze betraying her confusion. "What happened yesterday? Why did that vinyl trigger such a reaction? I need to know."

Margaret looked away. "I already told you, some things are better left unknown. Now, have some coffee; I just made it," she said, handing her a full cup of coffee.

Bet understood that her mother was hiding something. Their relationship had always been superficial, and they never truly talked about how they felt in difficult situations. Bet had always turned to her father for that—he had a natural ability to read her moods with just a look. With him, Bet never had to explain herself; he just knew what was in her heart.

With her mother, things were harder. She was impenetrable, like a concrete wall. But this time, Bet noticed something different in Margaret's eyes —there was a melancholy that betrayed deep pain tied to something Bet couldn't grasp. She also knew that now, it was her responsibility to take care of her mother when no one else could. Bet had returned to Richmond for that reason, determined to make up for the time she had been absent and to forgive her mother for being harsh. She was ready to listen and hoped her mother would finally open up.

Margaret's expression grew darker, a single tear running down her cheek as she finished preparing the eggs, wiping her face with the back of her hand in a barely noticeable motion to avoid Bet's gaze.

"Mom, what's wrong?" Bet asked, her voice as gentle as possible. "I know you and I have never really talked, especially since Dad died. But I came all the way from New York for you, and if I didn't care about you, I wouldn't be here. I know something strange is happening, and I can feel you're hiding something important from me. Please, tell me what's going on so I can help."

Margaret turned off the stove and collapsed into a fit of sobbing, curling into herself. Bet stood up and gently placed a hand on her mother's shoulder. "Come on, let's sit on the couch," Bet said.
Margaret dragged herself, sobbing, to the couch, struggling to breathe.
"Tell me everything," Bet urged, supporting her.

"Your father," Margaret whispered, her voice barely audible, as if she were struggling to get the words out. "The record... that record. You must never listen to it! That vinyl brings death and darkness, and anyone who comes into contact with it..." Margaret couldn't finish her sentence. Her hands trembled as she covered her eyes, trying to block out the horror of her memories.

Bet couldn't understand. "What does the record have to do with Dad?"

Margaret didn't respond, but her face was etched with immense pain. Tears streamed down her cheeks. Bet had never seen her mother like this. She hugged her tightly, determined to get to the bottom of the story.

Bet tried calling James, but there was no signal. She decided she'd visit him later, but first, she wanted to take a drive through the town to figure out what was happening.

Bet left the house with a heavy heart, feeling a growing unease she couldn't explain. The chirping of the cicadas had become a constant background noise, a sound that seemed to worm its way into her mind, growing louder with every step she took toward the car. The suffocating summer heat blanketed the town, making the atmosphere feel oppressive. Bet sensed an unusual tension in the air, as if something invisible was warping the atmosphere around her.

When she started the car, the engine sputtered twice before coming to life. Bet's heart raced as the vehicle hesitated, resisting the idea of starting. It was just an old car, but the timing couldn't have been worse for a breakdown. When the engine finally roared to life, Bet released a breath she hadn't realized she was holding and drove off slowly, trying to shake the lingering unease that was gnawing at her. She decided to head to the library, hoping for some peace and maybe some answers.

As she drove through Richmond, Bet immediately noticed something was off. It wasn't the usual scenes of everyday life she had come to expect; there was something unsettling about everything she saw.

The streets, normally filled with people chatting or rushing about their errands, were almost deserted. The few people Bet did see were moving strangely, as if disconnected from the reality around them.

A familiar figure caught her attention: Sarah Miller, a woman Bet had known her whole life, a model of grace and composure, was standing at the entrance of Richmond's old church. Her figure seemed out of place, like a distorted shadow against the church's massive doors. Bet stopped and looked closer, noticing with horror that one of Sarah's legs hung unnaturally, visibly broken, with the skin turning bluish and bruised. But what sent a chill through Bet's veins was the expression on Sarah's face: a disturbing smile, almost ecstatic, as she clutched the church door handle as if she were ready to enter.

Bet felt an overwhelming urge to intervene, but something held her back. Sarah was swaying back and forth, murmuring some sort of incomprehensible prayer, the words spilling from her lips without meaning. Occasionally, her body shuddered as if seized by a tremor, but she seemed completely unaware of the severity of her injury. Bet noticed that Sarah's broken foot barely touched the ground, swinging in a grotesque motion with each movement. The scene had an air of unreality, like Bet was watching a disturbing painting.

Suddenly, Sarah's smile twisted into a grin, and she made a sound Bet couldn't interpret—a mix of laughter and a sob. Bet's heart pounded in her chest, and she realized she couldn't stay there.

Driven by a growing sense of terror, she restarted the car and drove away quickly, trying to erase that chilling vision from her mind.

As she continued toward the library, Bet realized that the madness creeping through the town wasn't limited to a few individuals. Turning down a side street, she saw Mrs. Anderson, an elderly widow she had known all her life, standing next to her grandson. The boy, who Bet remembered as lively and kind, now stood completely still, his gaze lost in the distance. His arms hung stiffly by his sides, and blood trickled from the base of his ears, staining the collar of his white shirt.

Bet slowed down, her breath growing short as she watched the surreal scene. Mrs. Anderson, usually sweet and caring, was now shouting at her grandson with a ferocity Bet had never imagined her capable of. Her words were filled with rage, curses that hurt just to hear. But what was even more disturbing was the boy's lack of reaction. He showed no emotion, as if he didn't feel either the pain or the screaming. His eyes were empty, his gaze fixed on some faraway point, as though his mind had already left.

Bet felt a wave of nausea wash over her. She couldn't comprehend how this was possible. Despite her instinct to intervene, fear held her back. It was as though part of her knew she couldn't help the boy, that something terribly wrong was happening, and she wasn't capable of stopping it. With her heart in her throat, she sped away from the scene, feeling the weight of despair growing inside her.

Just before reaching the library, Bet witnessed another unsettling scene. Amelia Anderson, a young mother Bet had known for years, was furiously shaking a stroller as she walked down the street. Amelia's face was twisted in a ferocious expression, a sneer Bet had never seen on her before. And the noise… a baby's wailing filled the air, heartbreaking and sharp.

Bet decided to intervene. Amelia had never shown signs of violence, and her behavior was completely out of the ordinary. She parked the car and cautiously approached, her heart pounding in her chest. "Amelia, is everything okay?" she asked, her voice trembling more than she'd intended.

Amelia didn't answer immediately, continuing to shake the stroller as if she were entirely absorbed in that action. When she finally looked up, her eyes were glassy, unseeing. "I can't make him stop..." she whispered in a broken, almost mechanical voice. "He never stops crying..."

Bet felt a shiver of terror run down her spine. She leaned in to look inside the stroller, expecting to find a baby in the throes of a crying fit. But the stroller was empty. Bet's eyes widened in disbelief. The crying continued, but there was no baby.

Was she losing her mind too? Bet recoiled, confused and frightened, as the baby's cries mingled with the incessant chirping of the cicadas, creating an infernal echo in her mind. She brought a hand to her forehead, trying to make sense of her thoughts, but it was as though a fog had descended over her mind, making everything blurry and oppressive.

Amelia, meanwhile, seemed to have slipped into a trance, her movements becoming increasingly violent. Without warning, she hurled the empty stroller against the wall with surprising strength, the remains of plastic and metal scattering across the pavement. " I Cant make him stop!" she screamed, her voice sounding as though it came from an abyss of despair.

The scream made Bet jump back, her heart pounding in her chest. It was too much for her. The surreal scene was suffocating her. She rushed back to the car, her hands trembling as she tried to fit the key into the ignition. The engine sputtered, refusing to start. Panic surged within her, but she kept turning the key with determination until finally, the engine roared to life. Casting one last glance at Amelia, who was now collapsed on the ground, sobbing silently, Bet hit the gas, fleeing from that infernal scene.

Bet arrived at the library, her heart racing. The relentless chirping of the cicadas had burrowed into her mind, like a nightmare she couldn't escape. She parked the car hastily, her hands still shaking as she turned off the engine. Without taking a moment to calm herself, she rushed toward the library entrance, her steps quick and frantic.

The library doors creaked open, and Bet stepped inside, quickly shutting out the outside world and the obsessive sound of the cicadas. Inside, the silence was almost surreal—a brief moment of relief that gave her a false sense of security. She took a deep breath, trying to calm her frantic heartbeat, but the anxiety wouldn't subside.

Emily Ross, the librarian, was arranging some books on the shelves near the front desk when she turned and noticed Bet. At first, a warm smile spread across her face, but it quickly faded when she saw the expression on Bet's face.

"Bet?" Emily asked, her voice full of surprise and concern. "What are you doing here? It's been so many years..."

Bet tried to respond, but the words caught in her throat. She couldn't tell if what she had seen on the streets was real or if her mind was unraveling under the pressure of something incomprehensible.

She felt as though she was on the verge of collapsing, as if madness was creeping up inside her.

Emily studied her carefully, noting how pale Bet looked and how her hands trembled. She stepped closer, her face full of concern. "Bet, what happened? Are you alright?"

Bet ran a hand over her face, trying to find some clarity. "I don't know…" she whispered, her voice barely audible. "Emily, I… I've seen things… things I can't explain."

Emily took another step closer, her expression filled with genuine concern. "What did you see, Bet? You can talk to me. I'm here to listen."

Bet hesitated, doubting whether she was losing her grip on reality. Everything she had witnessed— Sarah's broken leg, the blood streaming from Mrs. Anderson's grandson's ears, Amelia and the empty stroller—seemed like scenes from a nightmare. Speaking them out loud might make them real, and she feared losing control of her mind completely.

"I don't know if I should," she finally admitted, shaking her head slightly. "It's all so… absurd. I'm afraid I'm going insane."

Emily placed a comforting hand on her arm. "You're not crazy, Bet. Richmond has always had its secrets. There are things in this town that many don't know about, ancient things that most people have forgotten… or chosen to ignore. People are starting to act strange. I've noticed it too."

Bet looked up, her eyes wide with fear. "What are you talking about?"
Emily guided her toward one of the chairs near the front desk, gesturing for her to sit. Then, with a grave expression, she began to speak in a low voice. "Richmond has a dark history, Bet. There are stories, legends, that go back a long way. It's said that the land this town is built on is cursed, haunted by forces that awaken every so often, bringing with them… chaos and madness."

Bet slumped in her chair, trying to process what she was hearing. "But what does that have to do with what I saw? With what's happening now?"
Emily nodded slowly, as if she had expected the question. "The cicadas, Bet. Have you noticed how loud their sound has been this year?"

Bet stiffened, connecting the dots. "Yes, it's unbearable. I can't get rid of that sound."

"It's a sign," Emily continued. "Every time these... forces awaken, the cicadas start to chirp in a strange way, as if they're being driven by something malevolent. The sound is so persistent, it feels like it's trying to drive you mad. And this isn't the first time it's happened."

Bet felt a chill run down her spine. "What else do you know, Emily?"

Emily stood and walked over to one of the older shelves in the library, returning with a heavy book, its cover worn and yellowed with age. "There are old records, stories passed down over time. They talk about a similar phenomenon that occurred many years ago. The cicadas, the chaos... and then people start changing, behaving strangely, as if they're losing their humanity."

Bet stared at the book, her mind racing to connect everything she had seen and heard. "Is this sound... connected to everything that's happening in town?"

"It seems so, based on what I've been able to understand," Emily replied, her face etched with worry. "And that's why we need to be careful. We need to figure out what's happening before it's too late."

Bet ran a hand through her hair, still in disbelief. She hesitated for a moment before confessing what she had found. "There's something else, Emily. A few days ago, I went into an old record store… I don't even know why I went in, but I found a vinyl. It was old, dusty, and I shouldn't have even touched it, but I took it."

Emily's eyes narrowed with concern. "What kind of vinyl?"

Bet swallowed, the memory of the record sending a growing sense of unease through her. "The title is The Sound of the Cicadas. The cover shows a forest… and in the background, a dark cave, hidden among shadows. When I saw it, I couldn't help but feel it was all connected."

Emily remained silent for a moment, her face growing more serious. "And what did you do with that vinyl, Bet?"

"I asked James, an old friend, to take a look. He's always been a music expert, and I thought he could tell me more. But… when we tried to listen to it, something strange happened."

Emily leaned forward, clearly alarmed. "What happened?"

Bet ran a hand across her forehead, trying to piece together her thoughts. "We started hearing the cicadas, but it was different… more intense, more… alive. And then, suddenly, we both passed out. When we woke up, the vinyl was still spinning, but the needle wasn't on the record anymore. James says he saw something while he was out… a vision of a forest and a cave. The same image that's on the record's cover and the same one I saw."

Emily sat still, her face pale. "You should never have touched that record, Bet. It could be connected to what's happening here. What you've described is not normal. The cicadas, the visions… all of this could be part of something much bigger, something ancient and dangerous."

Bet felt overwhelmed, the reality of Emily's words hitting her like a punch. "I don't know what to do, Emily. I feel like everything is spinning out of control."

Emily took a deep breath, trying to stay calm. "We need to learn more. Before it's too late. There's a book that might help us; it talks about the cicadas and their role in certain phenomena. Maybe it will give us some clue about what's happening here."

Bet nodded, fighting to keep the rising panic at bay. "Please, let's find it."

Emily stood and led her to a darker section of the library, where the oldest and rarest books were kept. She returned with a heavy, ancient-looking volume, its leather cover worn by time. "This book might contain what we're looking for. But Bet, whatever happens, we need to be careful. Richmond is changing, and that record may be the key to understanding what's happening."

Bet took the book with trembling hands, feeling that each passing minute was bringing her closer to something terrible. She needed answers, but she also knew that what she uncovered might push her even closer to the edge of madness.

Chapter 6: The Secrets of Richmond

Bet and Emily immersed themselves in the ancient book, a heavy tome with yellowed pages and a worn leather cover. The silence of the library, interrupted only by the distant chirping of cicadas, created an atmosphere of tension as they flipped through the pages, searching for answers.

The first thing they found was a detailed story about the construction of the library itself. "Look here!" said Emily, pointing to a paragraph written in tiny, precise handwriting.

"Benjamin Henry Latrobe was a renowned British-American engineer and architect, famous for his work in designing iconic buildings in the United States, such as the U.S. Capitol in Washington, D.C., and the Baltimore Cathedral. Latrobe was a man of great ingenuity and intellectual depth, with an interest in science, mathematics, and classical architecture, but also in more esoteric theories, such as sacred geometry."

Bet leaned in, reading with growing curiosity. "What brought him to Richmond?"

"Latrobe was called to Richmond after a wave of collective madness devastated the city about 200 years ago. The local authorities, desperate to find a solution, sought out a man capable of understanding not only engineering and architecture but also the darker mysteries related to the earth and sound. Latrobe was known not only for his architectural skills but also for his interest in sacred geometry and esoteric theories."

Emily continued reading, her voice tense. "Latrobe was fascinated by sacred geometry and the possibility that certain shapes and structures could influence human behavior and even contain or repel dark forces. He designed the Richmond library with these principles in mind. The thick, angled walls, the precisely positioned windows, and the geometric forms that break and absorb sound waves were all part of a plan to create a safe haven against the evil that seemed to dwell beneath the city."

Bet paused for a moment to reflect, then resumed reading. The following pages spoke of how Latrobe had discovered ancient documents and esoteric texts that mentioned dark presences linked to the chirping of the cicadas. Latrobe believed that the land beneath Richmond was infused with a kind of negative energy, which could be activated by certain sounds or rituals.

"Emily, look at this," said Bet, her voice tense. "Latrobe believed that these presences could be contained or neutralized by using sacred geometry and specific sound frequencies. He built the library as a sort of acoustic trap, a place where sound couldn't penetrate and where people could be protected from the malignant influence of the cicadas."

Emily nodded. "Latrobe knew that mere physical protection wouldn't be enough. He used ancient techniques and knowledge to create this sanctuary in Richmond, a place designed to withstand the dark forces that seemed to reside in the city."

As they continued reading, Bet and Emily found further references to an ancient phonograph cylinder Latrobe had mentioned in his notes. The cylinder, created by a secret sect operating in Richmond, contained a ritual that could, if performed correctly, seal the dark presences that awakened cyclically.

Bet pointed to a passage in the book. "This phonograph cylinder... Latrobe believed it could hold the key to sealing those presences. But he warned that if it were listened to improperly, it could have the opposite effect, awakening them and unleashing chaos."

Emily leaned forward, her face marked with concern. "And that vinyl record you found could be a copy of that cylinder. Someone must have recorded that ritual onto the vinyl... but if they didn't know what they were doing, they could have compromised everything."

Bet stopped, a thought beginning to form in her mind. "Who could have done it? Who would have had access to such an ancient phonograph cylinder

and known how to transfer it to vinyl?"

Emily seemed to ponder for a moment, then an expression of realization crossed her face. "There was a man... the owner of the record shop. His name was Richard Miller. He was a strange type, very reserved, but he had an obsessive passion for musical relics. He always said he wanted to preserve the history of music, at any cost. He jealously guarded his record collection, refusing to sell certain pieces to anyone he didn't deem worthy."

A chill ran down Bet's spine. "You said his name was Richard Miller? Do you know what happened to him?"

Emily shook her head, her expression somber. "He disappeared a few years ago, shortly after closing the shop. I don't know much else, only that one day he just left without a trace. But before he left, some people said he started acting strangely, talking about sounds only he could hear and presences that were haunting him."

Bet nodded slowly, the pieces of the puzzle beginning to fit together. "Miller... that name sounds familiar. Wasn't he connected to one of the most respected families in Richmond?"

"Yes," replied Emily. "The Millers, along with the Rhoads, founded one of the largest department stores in Richmond in 1885. Miller & Rhoads became an institution in the city, known for its quality and its connection to the community. However, Richard Miller was different. He distanced himself from the family business, focusing on his darker passions. Not much was said about him, except for his strange behavior and his obsession with collecting old records and relics."

Bet reflected on this information, feeling the weight of Richmond's history pressing on her, along with her responsibility for her mother's safety. She couldn't let anything happen to her. "I have to call my mother and tell her she's no longer safe in that house. The library is the safest place for her."

Emily nodded, the worry evident on her face. "Do it quickly, Bet. The situation in the city is getting worse by the minute."

Bet stood up, determined. "Thank you, Emily." She quickly grabbed her phone from her leather backpack, but the display showed clear signs of malfunction. "Damn! Just what I needed!"

With her heart pounding in her chest, Bet ran out of the library and headed for her mother's house. The chirping of the cicadas had become an almost omnipresent sound, and the air seemed to vibrate under its pressure. As she ran, her thoughts raced toward Richard Miller and what he might have done to provoke all of this.

She arrived at the house to find Margaret still sitting, pale and confused. Bet approached her, taking her hands. "Mom, we need to go. We're not safe!"

Margaret looked at her with eyes full of uncertainty. "Why?"

Bet smiled at her, trying to instill confidence. "Don't worry, Mom. I'll explain everything, but we have to move now. The library is safer."

Bet helped her mother up and calmly guided her to the car parked outside. Once they were both seated inside the vehicle, Bet tried to keep calm as she inserted the key into the ignition. The silence inside the car was oppressive, broken only by the chirping of the cicadas, which seemed to besiege the car from outside.

She turned the key, but the engine didn't respond immediately. The silence grew heavier, and Bet felt a wave of panic and heat wash over her. She tried again, but the engine coughed and died.

"Mom, everything will be fine!" Bet said, trying to mask the tension in her voice. Margaret nodded, seemingly unaware of her daughter's growing anxiety.

Bet closed her eyes for a moment, taking a deep breath. When she opened them again, she saw something that made her jump. Standing directly in front of the car was a figure, motionless. It was an old man, but there was something profoundly disturbing about his presence. He wore dirty, ragged clothes, and his face was contorted in an expression of pure hatred.

Bet felt her blood run cold. The man didn't move, staring at the car with glassy eyes and a slowly widening, malevolent smile.

Suddenly, without warning, the man began pounding his fists on the hood of the car, shouting something incomprehensible—a sort of guttural wail that seemed to come from the depths of his soul.

Bet tried to remain calm, but her heart was pounding furiously. She turned the key again, and this time, the engine roared to life. With a quick motion, Bet shifted the car into gear and slammed on the gas, trying to get away from the unsettling scene as fast as possible.

The noise of the cicadas seemed to intensify as they drove away, and Bet couldn't help but glance in the rearview mirror. The man was still there, standing in the middle of the street, his glassy stare and sinister grin foreboding something terrible.

As she drove toward the library, Bet focused on the road, ignoring the deafening chirping and the memory of the man who seemed determined to stop her from bringing her mother to safety.

Margaret's expression was blank, clearly in a state of confusion. After what felt like an eternity, they finally arrived in front of the library.

Bet sighed in relief when she saw Emily at the entrance, ready to welcome them. With trembling hands, she helped her mother out of the car and quickly guided her into the safety of the building.

"We're safe here!" Bet whispered to her mother, trying to reassure her while Emily helped them inside.

Now that Margaret was safe, Bet knew she had to return to her mission. Clutching the ancient book in her hands, she headed back to her car. She had to find James and figure out what to do with the vinyl, but she also knew that finding Richard Miller would be crucial.

Chapter 7: The Search for Answers

Bet left the library, her heart still racing from everything she had discovered. Emily's words echoed in her mind: the library had been built as an acoustic trap, a refuge against the dark forces lurking beneath Richmond. Then there was the name Richard Miller, the man who had once owned the record store. A man who, according to Emily, had distanced himself from his respectable family to follow a darker path.

As she drove toward James' house, the cicadas' chirping seemed to intensify, as if they were following her, enveloping her in a sonic veil that threatened her sanity. Bet tried to ignore the incessant sound, focusing instead on memories of James, the boy she had always admired, now a man—still a brilliant but struggling musician. She recalled the days when she would sit for hours, listening to him play, dreaming that one day he might notice her feelings for him. And now, as the world seemed to fall apart, James was perhaps the only person she could still trust.

She finally arrived at James' house. The small suburban home, surrounded by trees sagging under the weight of the heat, was an oasis amidst the madness consuming Richmond. Bet parked the car and hurried to the door, clutching the ancient book tightly in her hands.

James greeted her with a smile that, for a moment, made her forget everything that was happening. But a quick glance into his eyes revealed that he, too, felt the tension in the air. However, there was something strange about his behavior. His movements were jittery, and his gaze, which until the previous day had been steady and confident, now seemed distracted, as if he were battling something within himself.

"Bet, you made it just in time! I tried calling, but all the phone lines are down, and the devices seem to be malfunctioning," James said, ushering her inside. "I spent all night working on that vinyl. I've discovered something really disturbing."

As Bet followed him into the recording studio, she couldn't help but notice how much James had changed since the previous day. His behavior fluctuated, swinging between moments of apparent calm and sudden bursts of anger or euphoria. It was as though working on that vinyl had affected him, as if something had struck him, making him unrecognizable.

"James, are you alright?" Bet asked, trying to hide the concern in her voice.

"Yes, yes, I'm fine!" James replied, a bit too quickly. Then, with an abrupt shift in tone, he added more darkly, "At least... I think so."

Bet struggled not to show her unease and followed him into the studio. The room was small but well-equipped, filled with state-of-the-art gear that James had assembled over the years, piece by piece. On the table, next to a mixer and a computer, lay the vinyl he had found in the abandoned record store. Just seeing it there, in the dimly lit room, sent shivers down her spine.

Next to the vinyl was an open notebook, filled with handwritten notes James had made over the years. Bet recognized it immediately: it was the notebook where James, ever since he was a boy, had jotted down all his research and experiments on sound frequencies and how they interacted with the human body. The notebook had a black leather cover, worn by time, but what made it unmistakable was the intricate spiral James had drawn as a teenager—hypnotic, with interwoven lines creating an almost three-dimensional effect. Bet remembered how proud James had been of that drawing and how he had chosen it to represent the whirlwind of ideas swirling in his mind. That spiral, now faded but still visible, symbolized his endless passion for music and its hidden potentials.

"I always knew frequencies could do more than just produce sound," James said, absentmindedly flipping through the notebook's pages. "I've spent years trying to figure out how certain frequencies can affect the human brain—how they can either calm or agitate it, depending on how they're used."

James pointed to a page in the notebook, where various notes on sound frequencies and their effects on the human body were scribbled. "See this part?" he said, his voice low and troubled.

"Frequencies between 50 and 60 hertz seem harmless, like the faint hum you barely notice from an old appliance. But if amplified, they can become incredibly insidious."

He paused, struggling to find the right words to convey his growing anxiety. "Under normal conditions, these frequencies can start interfering with the nervous system, causing disorientation, anxiety, and even nausea. It's like they force your body to vibrate to their rhythm, creating a malaise you just can't shake off."

He stepped closer to Bet, concern etched on his face. "Now imagine being exposed to these frequencies for a long period. At first, you might not even notice and just feel a slight discomfort. But over time, you'd start feeling increasingly nervous, unable to focus, like your mind is constantly under siege. This vibration doesn't stop at your head—it spreads through your body like an invisible wave coursing through your muscles and tissues, making you feel like you're losing control."

He pointed to another part of the notebook, his fingers trembling slightly. "The worst part is when these frequencies begin resonating inside you, as if they're tuning into the most delicate parts of your body. At first, it's just a tingling sensation, but then it becomes something far more disturbing. It's as if every fiber of your being is pushed to the breaking point, destabilizing you completely from the inside."

James looked at her gravely. "That's what terrifies me, Bet. If these frequencies have been intentionally combined with the sound of the cicadas, they could devastate anyone who listens to them. This isn't just an unpleasant sound—it's an invisible force that could slowly unravel a person, until they lose all control over themselves."

James gestured toward the frequency analyzer screen he had turned on. "Look at this," he said, pointing to a series of peaks dancing on the display. "I analyzed the vinyl using the frequency analyzer. Normally, a vinyl has many frequencies that make up music, but this... this is different. There are only two distinct frequency groups."

Bet stepped closer, watching the graphs on the screen. "Two groups of frequencies?"

James nodded, a disturbing smile that didn't reach his eyes forming on his lips. "Yes. The primary frequencies are the ones you hear most clearly — they hover around 4500 hertz. Interestingly, this is the same average frequency produced by cicadas when they chirp in groups. These high frequencies create a continuous tension, almost as if they're trying to keep the listener in a constant state of alertness. But then there are these..." He pointed to another peak on the graph, much lower, dominating the screen. "These are much lower frequencies, between 50 and 60 hertz. They're more subtle, less perceptible to the human ear, but they're there... and they're powerful."

"What does it mean?" Bet asked, her voice betraying her unease.

"I'm not sure," James replied, his brow furrowed as he tried to piece together his thoughts. "But I believe these lower frequencies contain the real message. When I isolated them, I found they seem to carry words, but they're distorted... as if they were recorded during some kind of ritual, along with the cicadas themselves. I can't fully decipher them yet, but it sounds ancient, something that doesn't belong to this time."

A chill ran down Bet's spine. "Words recorded in a ritual along with the cicadas? Like some sort of incantation?"

"Exactly," James replied with a very serious expression. But then, with a sudden outburst, he turned toward her, his eyes wide, almost crazed. "And that would explain why whoever recorded this vinyl went insane. If they really transferred these frequencies from an old phonograph cylinder, they could have awakened something dark... something that should never have been disturbed."

Bet sat down, the weight of everything they had discovered beginning to press down on her. "So, what do we do now? How do we stop this?"

James ran a hand through his hair, his movements frantic, almost feverish. He rifled through his notes as he continued speaking to Bet, "We need to decode the full message. It might tell us how to reverse the process, how to seal those presences back. But there's a problem... I'm not sure I have the right equipment to do it here. We might need help."

"Who can we ask?" Bet asked, her voice edged with desperation.

"I know someone at Virginia Commonwealth University," James replied, his voice now calm, almost whispering, but with a shadow of something dark. "Here it is!" James said, waving a small card he found among his notes, "Professor Thomas Wakefield. He's an expert in anthropology and folklore. He's one of the brightest, and also one of the most eccentric, professors in the department.

Wakefield is known for his passion for ancient rituals and his collection of esoteric artifacts. He's the kind of person who immerses himself completely in his work—some say he lives more in the past than in the present. He might even have the equipment we need to better analyze these frequencies and decode the words. We have to find him!"

Bet nodded, feeling a new sense of hope. But she couldn't shake the feeling that something was wrong with James. Something was changing in him, and the thought that the vinyl might be causing all of this filled her with deep unease. "We need to go, now," she said, looking at James with concern. The thought of losing him now, after finally reconnecting, gripped her heart with fear.

She had never had a deeper connection with anyone than she had with James, where, ever since she was young, she could be herself without worrying about appearances—the only person she felt she could share her worries with without being judged. But after her father's death, she had hardened her heart with grief, vowing never to show her vulnerability to anyone again.

But now, her heart was racing at the thought that something might go wrong. *What if I never get the chance to tell him what I feel for him?* she thought, hesitating over whether to speak or not. But there was no time. They had to go.

Chapter 8: The University

Bet and James found themselves engulfed in the darkest night Richmond had ever seen. The cicadas' chirping, which during the day had been an eerie anthem of despair, had now turned into a deafening cacophony, as if it were trying to overwhelm them. Every buzz, every hiss seemed to pierce their brains like an invisible blade, trying to shatter their sanity.

Bet's Ford struggled along the deserted streets, the engine vibrating as though it might give out under the oppressive atmosphere. James sat beside her, staring out the window, trying to fend off the rising panic. Every so often, the flickering streetlights illuminated scenes that looked like something out of a nightmare.

The streets were empty, but not dead. Here and there, Bet and James glimpsed figures moving in the shadows, hunched under an invisible weight, as if something had drained their very life essence.

The buildings loomed like blackened skeletons, their open windows revealing only darkness and desolation. But what struck them most was what lay along the sides of the road.

"Look there," James said in a low voice, pointing to the sidewalk.

Bet followed his gaze and saw a dead dog, its body stiff, its ears stained with dark blood. Further ahead, a cat lay in an unnatural position, its ears also oozing blood. Horror quickly spread as Bet had to swerve abruptly to avoid a group of dead birds scattered like dry leaves on the road.

"It's the sound!" James whispered, his face pale. "It's killing everything it touches."

Bet nodded, her throat tightening with anguish. There was no need to speak; they both knew that what was happening was something far beyond them. The entire city seemed to have fallen into an endless nightmare, and they were trapped in the middle of it.

As they drove, the cicadas' chirping seemed to intensify, as though someone or something was orchestrating that infernal screeching. The car passed by a playground, where the swings swayed gently, pushed by an illusory wind. The shadows stretching along the building walls seemed to come alive, twisting into spectral forms before vanishing in the car's headlights.

Every now and then, Bet caught a reflection in the mirrors, as if some entity were watching them from the darkness. But whenever she turned to look, there was nothing. Only that damned sound, growing louder and more intrusive with every passing second. The night offered no relief from the suffocating heat, making the air almost unbreathable.

Finally, the outline of the Virginia Commonwealth University buildings appeared on the horizon. But instead of providing a sense of safety, the university seemed like a place abandoned even by God. The buildings were shrouded in an unnatural darkness, lost within their own shadows.

"It's like the city is dead," Bet said, turning off the engine. "Let's go, we have to find Professor Walker."

Bet and James slipped out of the car, and the cicadas' chirping immediately wrapped around them like a suffocating shroud. Each step felt heavier than the last as they made their way to the university's main entrance. Once inside, they were greeted by a sense of foreboding; the hallways were deserted, but there were clear signs of recent chaos. Overturned desks, books scattered everywhere, red stains on the walls, and footprints —some in blood—marked the floor.

Instinctively, James led Bet toward the classroom where he knew Professor Walker held his lectures. Walker was the only person James had thought to turn to, given his expertise in psychology, neurology, and acoustic physics applied to sound and its interaction with the human body.

Suddenly, Bet felt a knot tighten in her stomach. She hadn't set foot in this building since she had finished her studies and decided to leave Richmond. The memories gripped her heart, making her feel as though she was reliving the last months before she left, that damned afternoon in the library, studying. She didn't want to make space for the pain and fought with all her strength to focus on the real reason she was there. But the words she had heard from her mother in that phone call kept echoing in her mind, as she stared incredulously at the black-and-white checkered floor of the library, tears falling almost rhythmically onto her burgundy leather shoes. "Your father…" Margaret had said in a trembling voice on the other end of the line, "There was nothing they could do…"

"Bet!" James called, shaking her slightly. "We have to keep moving."

Bet blinked, her eyes swollen with tears, and continued down the long hallway with James.

The neon lights flickered, casting sinister shadows along the corridors, and the university was far from silent; that incessant buzzing, amplified by the empty halls and classrooms, reverberated like an unstoppable wave, threatening to overwhelm them once again. Every step the two of them took seemed to disappear, swallowed by the noise and the pounding sound that filled the air.

"It's unbearable," Bet murmured, bringing her hands to her ears in a futile attempt to muffle the tormenting sound. "How can anyone endure this?"

James didn't respond, focused on trying to remember the way to Walker's classroom. The booming noise seemed to follow them everywhere, invading every corner of the building with an oppressive and menacing energy.

As they advanced down the hallway, they noticed something that made them shudder: blood stains scattered on the floor, as if someone had been injured and tried to flee. These traces led directly to Walker's classroom door, which was slightly ajar, with a faint light filtering from within.

"This doesn't look good," Bet whispered, her heart beginning to race.

James nodded, approaching the door cautiously. When he gently pushed it open, the door creaked, revealing the classroom inside. The scene before them was chilling in its simplicity.

The floor was marked by sporadic bloodstains, but there were no bodies or signs of a violent struggle,

as though the students had fled in panic, leaving behind a sense of chaos and despair. The walls, only partially smeared with blood, gave the impression of a place where fear had taken over.

"This... is a nightmare," Bet whispered, her heart pounding in her chest. "What the hell happened here?"

James approached one of the desks, staring at the scene with wide eyes. "I don't know, but Walker's not here. If he were, he wouldn't have panicked like the others. I know him too well—he must've found somewhere safe."

Bet turned to him, her mind racing. "Where could he have gone? There's nowhere safe in this damned building."

James seemed to think deeply, resting his head in his hands, and then his face suddenly lit up. "The soundproof room! The one used for Acoustic Psychology and Neuroscience tests... Walker's the only one with the keys. If he's taken refuge anywhere, it's there."

Bet nodded, feeling a faint glimmer of hope rise within her. "Let's go, we have to find him before it's too late."

Finally, Bet and James reached the room, one of the few places designed to be completely isolated from external noise. The door was thick, reinforced to ensure maximum acoustic protection. James knocked hard, hoping the professor was still inside, safe and sound.

"Professor Walker! It's James, I'm here with my friend Bet! We need to speak with you!" James called out, his heart pounding in his chest.

There was a moment of silence, then a crack appeared, and a pair of tired, wary eyes peered out at them. "Who are you? What do you want?" asked a voice filled with fear and suspicion.

"We came to ask for your help, professor!" James replied, trying not to sound too desperate, not wanting to scare him. "We're not like the others. We're still lucid."

The door opened slowly, revealing Professor Walker, visibly shaken but still sane. He wore a rumpled white lab coat, his hair was disheveled, and his eyes were rimmed with red, likely from overwork or whatever horrors he might have witnessed, though his large glasses hid them well.

"Come in, quickly!" Walker said, closing the door behind them. The room was enveloped in an almost surreal silence, the cicadas' chirping completely muffled by the thick soundproofed walls.

"We're safe from the sound in here," Walker explained, his voice weak and strained. "But we can't stay here for long. What's going on? Why have you sought me out? We need to get out of here."

James pulled the vinyl and the book from his bag, carefully placing them on the central table. Walker eyed them with a mix of curiosity and fear. "Where did you find this?" he asked, cautiously touching the vinyl's cover.

"In the old record store that Richard Miller owned," James replied. "We think it's connected to what's happening in the city."

Walker nodded slowly, recognizing the significance of what he had in front of him. His voice grew darker as he began to explain. "You're right to be concerned. This vinyl may have been just the catalyst, the medium for awakening something buried in Richmond for generations. But the vinyl isn't the real issue. The sound you're hearing, the noise that's overwhelming the entire city, is being amplified by something far older and more dangerous."

Bet and James exchanged alarmed glances as Walker quickly flipped through the old book, searching for a specific section.

"Two hundred years ago, Richmond was the site of a similar event," Walker continued. "The cicadas, the noise, the madness… it all originated from the caves in the forest north of the city. These caves are a unique geological phenomenon: they're primarily composed of limestone, a material known for its acoustic resonance properties. Inside, the stalactites and stalagmites create a natural amplification effect for sound."

Bet stared at him, incredulous. It all seemed so surreal: "So the cicadas' sound... is being amplified by these caves?"

"Exactly," Walker replied. "The cicadas are drawn to these caves, and their chirping, which is usually just annoying, becomes unbearably loud."

James, trying to piece together the puzzle, exclaimed, "And what does the vinyl have to do with this?"

"The vinyl and what's recorded on it are the key," Walker explained. "According to the book, in addition to a specific frequency very similar to that of the cicadas, there is also a ritual and specific words recorded that, when combined, induce the cicadas into an endless reproductive cycle, which continues even at night, when they would normally stop chirping."

Walker paused, then added, "But there's more. That ritual described in the book... seems to have been designed to reprogram the cicadas, causing their numbers to grow exponentially, driving people's minds to madness. That's why Richmond and its inhabitants are falling into the abyss of insanity."

"The caves," Walker continued, "were sealed a long time ago, blocking the sound and preventing an apocalyptic disaster. But now it seems that seal has been broken—perhaps accidentally, perhaps intentionally. The sound is growing, becoming unbearable for both people and animals, even miles away."

"But why now?" James asked, more confused than ever.

"I'm not sure," Walker admitted. "It's possible someone found the original phonograph cylinder mentioned in the book and transferred the recording onto the vinyl you found. This may have triggered the uncontrolled reproduction of the cicadas, breaking the balance that had been maintained for so long. Or natural causes, like tremors, might have shaken the seal, breaking it."

Bet shuddered in confusion, her mind struggling to connect the events and information. "So, what can we do? How can we stop all this?"

Walker looked at them both seriously. "The only solution may be to invert the frequencies, creating a phase cancellation device. Phase cancellation is a principle used in acoustics to cancel out an unwanted sound. Imagine two identical sound waves: if one of the waves is inverted, when the two waves meet, they cancel each other out. It's like one pushes while the other pulls equally. If we could invert the phase of the frequencies produced by the cicadas, we might—just might—neutralize the sound that's devastating the city."

James nodded, already thinking about how to build the device. "We'll need specific equipment, but it's possible."

Bet and James exchanged worried glances, knowing time was running out. As Walker prepared the equipment to analyze the vinyl, the soundproof room seemed to close in on them, as if the shadows were waiting for something to go wrong.

Walker carefully placed the vinyl on the turntable, which was connected to a sophisticated sound analysis system, making sure the speakers were disconnected. As the record began to spin, the frequencies started to emerge on the sound analyzer screen, tracing patterns and waves that seemed to dance on the edge of chaos.

"Stay focused," Walker said firmly, despite the rising tension. "What we're about to discover could change everything."

The surreal silence of the soundproof room offered temporary refuge from the chaos outside, but Bet and James knew it wouldn't last long. Time was running out, and with each passing second, they were drawing closer to a truth they would have preferred not to uncover.

The tension was palpable, the still air in the room creating a strange sensation for Bet, who had grown accustomed to the constant chirping of the cicadas. She didn't know what they would discover, and in the endless wait, her gaze met James'. She knew she could trust him.

Chapter 9: The Dark Revelations of Knowledge

The vinyl continued spinning on the turntable, and the distorted frequencies manifested on the screen like waves dancing over an unfathomable abyss, in front of Walker's wide, worried eyes. The glowing lines moved in seemingly meaningless patterns, yet Walker sensed that a terrible logic was emerging.

His face marked by concern, the professor closely observed the data scrolling across the screen. "This... this isn't just a random recording. The cicada sound has been manipulated and modulated along with the ritual etched into it. It's not just a natural call. From the emerging frequencies, it seems like some sort of sound impulse mixed in a way that destabilizes anyone unlucky enough to listen. But I need more elements to better understand the function of this sonic link. For now, it's best to transfer the track to my laptop. The file is key to stopping all this, but it won't be enough."

James approached the screen, his face a mask of concentration as he watched the macabre dance of what, at first glance, seemed like harmless frequencies. Bet could feel the tension growing within the group but knew they had to move quickly.

"And how do we build the device? Do we have everything we need?" Bet asked, breaking the silence heavy with anxiety.

Walker tore his gaze from the monitor and turned toward a metal cabinet in the corner of the soundproof room. "Good question," Walker said thoughtfully. "We can probably get some of the equipment here, but we'll need to head to the physics lab in hopes of finding the rest—amplifiers, wave generators, and proper acoustic speakers."

Bet and James exchanged a determined look. They knew time was running out.

Walker approached a shelf and grabbed three pairs of industrial protective headphones, the kind used to protect the ears from extremely loud noises. "Put these on," he said, handing them to Bet and James. "They won't offer total protection, but they'll help us endure the cicadas' sound and prevent us from losing our minds."

While Walker transferred the file from the vinyl to his laptop, Bet was the first to put on the headphones, her trembling hands adjusting them. She immediately noticed the near-total muffling of James and Walker's voices as they continued talking.

With the headphones secure, they gathered everything they needed and left the soundproof room.

Outside, the noise hit them like a physical blow, but the headphones were able to dampen it enough to allow them to press on, better protected from the devastating effects of the chirping. The oppressive heat engulfed them once again, the seasonal humidity intensifying with each step they took. The heat had become a constant presence in Richmond, an invisible enemy that added to the nightmare they were already living.

As they made their way through the university hallways, the chirping reverberating in their heads like a demonic concert, the flickering neon lights

above them trembled, some burned out, others flickering intermittently, casting unsettling shadows along their path. Sweat trickled down Bet's back, making her shirt stick to her skin, already drenched in dust and tension.

They reached the physics lab, and Walker, with a steady hand, opened the door despite the tension. Once inside, they immediately set to work, gathering amplifiers, acoustic speakers, cables, and sound wave generators. Every second was precious, and they knew that with every passing minute, Richmond was teetering closer to total madness.

The heat inside the lab was unbearable, the stagnant air making it difficult even to breathe. Walker suddenly stopped, his face tense as he tried to quickly recall what they might still need, though he managed to maintain a calm facade. "To complete the device, we'll need some technical manuals on applied sound physics. We need to check the university library!"

For Walker, the library held the hope of finding the missing information to complete the device. They loaded everything they'd gathered onto a mobile cart—usually used by students and teachers to transport equipment between classrooms for experiments—and headed toward the library, the headphones only partially dulling the deafening, persistent noise that followed them.

They crossed more corridors where the lights had completely gone out, leaving them enveloped in a suffocating darkness, broken only by the occasional flicker of functioning neon. The shadows seemed to lengthen and distort, following their movements like malevolent presences, and the persistent heat—an oppressive torment—added another layer of suffocation.

As they crossed one of the main hallways, Bet noticed a solitary figure slipping away from an open door. A young woman, perhaps a student, walked barefoot across the smooth floor, dragging her feet. Her hair was disheveled, and her gaze was fixed in a vacant stare. Bet slowed her pace, struck by the expression of total disorientation on the girl's face. She immediately noticed the girl's ears were dirty with blood, as though the sound had also torn her eardrums.

"James, wait," Bet whispered, stopping to watch the girl, her hands trembling uncontrollably.

James turned, following Bet's gaze. "What… who is that? Maybe we should…"

"Don't get too close," Walker shouted firmly. "Whoever she is, she's already gone too far. Look how she walks, like her body's disconnected from her mind."

Bet watched the girl for another moment, then felt a wave of sadness mixed with latent terror. "We can't just leave her like that…"

"We can't help her!" Walker shouted, grabbing Bet's arm to pull her along. "Madness has taken hold of many people here. If we stop, we risk getting pulled in too."

Suddenly, the young woman stopped, as if sensing Bet, James, and Walker's presence. She slowly turned toward them, her glassy eyes locking onto Bet's for a long, anguished moment. Then, without warning, she let out a scream that cut through even the cicadas' chirping and began running toward them, her hands stretched out like claws ready to tear them apart.

"Run!" Walker shouted, pushing the heavy cart filled with equipment. The young woman closed in fast, but her blind fury made her trip over some debris scattered in the hallway, sending her crashing to the ground. Still, she continued to scream as she frantically scrambled back to her feet, her movements unnatural and threatening as Bet and the others hurried to escape, trying to keep the heavy equipment from toppling off the cart.

"She won't stop!" Walker screamed, retreating with a pale face and wide eyes.

Acting on instinct, James noticed one of the electrical cables they had used for the equipment. Without thinking twice, he grabbed the thick, heavy cord and tossed it toward the girl, trying to entangle her legs.

The girl fell again, tripping over the cables, but this time the impact was more violent. Her head hit the floor with a dull thud, and for a moment, she lay still. However, with grotesque effort, she began trying to rise again, even though the cable held her legs firmly anchored to the floor.

"I can't believe it—she looks possessed," Bet whispered, her heart pounding wildly.

James couldn't let anyone harm Bet. Acting on pure instinct, he moved quickly toward the girl, grabbing the other end of the cable. With a swift, decisive motion, he wrapped the cord around her neck and pulled it tight. The girl thrashed violently, struggling to free herself, but her strength seemed to drain as the cable tightened around her throat.

James closed his eyes for a moment, trying not to think about what he was doing. "She had to stop..." he muttered to himself, feeling the girl's resistance slowly ebb away.

At last, the girl stopped moving. Her body collapsed to the floor, and the incessant chirping of the cicadas seemed to fade slightly, leaving only the sound of James's heavy breathing and the rapid pounding of his heart. His hands trembled, and for a moment, he stood frozen, staring at the girl's limp form on the floor. He had never harmed anyone, not even an insect, and the thought of what he had just done made him feel dirty. The instinct to protect Bet had taken over. The girl who had shared his childhood—the one who had always laughed at his silly jokes, who had held his hand for the first time in the park when he was seven and afraid to go home because his parents had fought the night before, the one he had sheltered from the storm with his jacket outside school when her umbrella broke, the one who had encouraged him at seventeen to play in public for the first time and followed all his quirks without ever judging him. He had to do it. He had to protect her at all costs.

James let go of the cable, his hands shaking, and took a step back. "We had no choice," Walker said as Bet looked at the girl with eyes full of horror and sadness.

"We need to leave now! There's no time to lose," Walker said, rewinding the cable and placing it back on the cart.

Bet took James's hand and pulled him away from the girl, just as she had in the park years ago, looking at him with eyes full of gratitude and regret. Without another word, the three of them resumed their race against time, leaving the lifeless body behind. But that terrible scene stayed with them, another mark of the horror consuming Richmond.

When they had put enough distance between them and the girl, they stopped to catch their breath. Bet was visibly trembling, and James couldn't take his eyes off the spot where they had left her.

"This is so wrong," Bet whispered, her voice breaking under the confusion. "It shouldn't have ended like that…"

Walker placed a hand on her shoulder. "This city is dying, Bet. We need to focus on what we can do. If we stop, we'll be lost too."

Bet nodded slowly, trying to calm herself as she watched James breathe heavily. Despair mingled with fear, but they had to keep going. They had to find a way to stop this.

They finally reached the university library, but the scene before them was desolate. The ancient wooden shelves, worn and shaky, had evidently succumbed to the sound. The relentless noise had caused the shelves to vibrate so violently that they had collapsed. The once neatly organized and precious books, as Bet remembered them, were now scattered across the floor in total chaos. Searching for the manuals they needed in this disaster would be impossible.

Bet was overwhelmed by despair. The place where her life had seemed to come to a halt years ago now lay catastrophically folded in on itself, as if the very environment had finally expressed all the pain Bet had been hiding in her heart over her father's death.

"We won't find anything here," she said, trying to keep calm and not let her memories slow her down. "We'll have to go to the city library. It's the safest place we have right now, and we'll probably find the manuals and books we need there. Besides, my mother is there, and I need to make sure she's okay," she added, thinking about the one person she had left to protect and care for.

Walker turned to Bet and James. "Where did you park your car? Where is it?"

"It's right in front of the university entrance," Bet replied, her tone slightly worried. "It's an old Ford, but it's been having trouble starting lately, that old junker."

Walker nodded decisively. "Then we'll load everything into my station wagon. I parked it in the professors' reserved lot behind the university. It'll take longer to get there, but it's the best option."

Bet and James nodded, knowing they had no other choice. They crossed the deserted hallways, each step a torment with the cicadas' screeching hammering in their heads, despite the protective headphones. The corridor lights flickered and went out, casting unsettling shadows along their path. Every shadow seemed to watch them, as if the darkness itself were conspiring against them.

At last, they reached the university exit and opened the door to the rear parking lot. The hot night air hit them like a wall, thick with the smell of dust and burnt oil. The professors' parking lot was shrouded in a spectral atmosphere, illuminated only by the flickering lights of a few still-functioning street lamps. Darkness dominated much of the space, while the yellowish beams of the lamps cast long, sinister shadows on the asphalt. The air was still and heavy, as though the oppressive heat had even stopped time. The cars were scattered haphazardly, many with shattered windows and doors left ajar, as if their owners had fled in haste, leaving behind chaos.

The ground was littered with shards of glass and debris, crunching beneath their feet. Here and there, abandoned bodies could be seen, some lying next to the cars, others slumped against the walls. Their faces were twisted in expressions of pain and terror, and from their ears, stained with dark blood, it was clear that the relentless sound had taken their last traces of sanity.

The silence between the three was broken only by the incessant chirping of the cicadas, a sound that seemed to come from every direction, amplified by the hard surfaces and empty corridors of the university. But aside from that infernal sound, they could hear another noise beneath their headphones: a low, rabid growl that seemed to emerge directly from the darkness of the shadows.

Suddenly, a movement caught the group's attention. Under the faint glow of a street lamp, a shadow moved quickly. Bet's heart leapt as she glimpsed the figure of a dog sprinting toward them. The dog, a dark gray pit bull, was covered in blood. Its eyes were completely white, gleaming with a wild madness under the flickering light. Its demonic growl, baring blood-stained teeth, was a clear sign that the animal had attacked someone— or something—in a fit of rage.

The pit bull stopped for a moment, watching the three, perhaps preparing its next attack.

Bet noticed that the dog's ears, too, were stained with blood, pulled back and ready to strike at the slightest provocation. The dog let out another low growl, a sound that seemed to vibrate in the hot, dense air of the parking lot, making them tense even more.

Sensing the imminent danger, Walker moved decisively, and with a swift motion, he grabbed a metal pipe from the equipment cart. "Bet, James, get behind me," he shouted, without taking his eyes off the dog.

Bet felt terror gripping her chest as the animal prepared to lunge at them. Walker waved the pipe, trying to keep the dog at bay.

The pit bull suddenly lunged forward, but Walker was ready. With a quick swing, he struck the dog with the pipe, sending it crashing to the ground with a muffled yelp. But the dog, consumed by blind fury, did not give up. It got back up and, with one final desperate move, sank its teeth into Walker's leg.

The dog's bite tightened with an inhuman strength, and blood began to pour freely. Seeing the situation, James rushed to grab the pipe and delivered a sharp blow to the pit bull's back, trying to force it to release its grip. The animal seemed possessed by a malignant force, continuing to bite down harder and harder. With a second blow, this time aimed at the head, James finally managed to stun the dog enough to make it collapse, unconscious.

Walker, visibly shaken and with his face contorted in pain, slumped against one of the abandoned cars. Bet wasted no time and rushed to another car with open doors, immediately noticing the blood-stained handle. Inside, she found a piece of light fabric on the back seat. She grabbed it and hurried back to Walker. Though Bet didn't know much about first aid, she used the fabric to momentarily press against the wound and try to stop the bleeding, but her heart pounded with anguish, and the blood covering her hands made everything more dramatic and slow.

"Walker, don't give up now!" Bet shouted, her voice filled with concern. "We need to get him out of here, now, James," she said. "Staying outside is too risky."

James nodded, and Walker tried to get back on his feet. "I can make it… but I can't drive in this condition."

James, still holding the bloodied pipe, put it back on the cart and bent down to help Walker up. "I'll drive. We need to move now."

With Walker limping and supported by James and Bet, the group finally made it to the station wagon. Carefully, James helped Walker into the back seat while Bet loaded the equipment into the trunk.

Once they had loaded all the necessary components, James climbed into the driver's seat. Bet sat in the back next to Walker, trying to tend to the wound, which seemed to have worsened. The blood had soaked the makeshift bandage she had used.

"Go, James," Bet said, her voice exhausted. "We don't have time to lose."

James started the engine, and the station wagon moved forward. As they left the parking lot, the cicadas' screeching seemed to grow in intensity, as though the city itself were trying to trap them in their own minds. The stifling heat inside the car seemed even worse, with the air barely circulating enough to relieve the oppressive discomfort.

The drive to the library was a nightmare. Richmond's streets were deserted, shrouded in darkness that seemed to absorb all hope. The cicadas' sound, though muffled by the headphones and the car's body, continued to hammer in their minds like an incessant mallet.

"We're almost there," James muttered, his voice tense. "We can't stop now."

Finally, the outline of the city library appeared on the horizon. The building's thick, solid walls seemed like a fortress against the chaos outside. James steered the station wagon toward the main entrance, trying to stay calm even though his heart was pounding in his chest. Bet pressed the cloth tightly against Walker's wound, trying to stop the bleeding as the car came to a stop in front of the entrance.

"We're here, finally," James exclaimed, his voice weary but filled with relief. He turned off the engine and looked at Bet. "Let's get Walker inside."

Bet nodded, opening the door and helping Walker out of the car. The professor limped badly, his face pale and clearly pained. With James's help, they managed to get him inside the library, where a wave of cool air and silence greeted them.

Margaret and Emily, who had stayed inside, immediately rushed over to them. "What happened?" Emily asked, seeing the blood dripping from Walker's leg.

"A crazed dog," Walker replied in a strained whisper. "But I'm fine... we have more important things to do."

James, Bet, and Walker all took off the suffocating headphones, which had been protecting them from losing their minds until now. What a relief they felt —the silence in the library was like an oasis of peace for their ears, battered by the journey and the incessant nightmare they had been living for far too long.

Emily wasted no time and ran to grab a first-aid kit she kept in the library for emergencies. She quickly returned and began tending to Walker's wound as best she could. Bet watched, trying to stay calm as the adrenaline slowly subsided, leaving her exhausted.

Walker allowed Emily to care for him in silence, gritting his teeth against the pain. When she finished disinfecting and bandaging his leg, she set Walker down in a chair, trying to give him some time to recover. Around him, the other survivors gathered, watching the scene with worried but determined expressions.

Meanwhile, James brought in all the equipment they had loaded into the car, but he was tired and needed a few minutes to process what had just happened.

Walker thanked Emily for her care, cleared his throat, and looked up at the group. "We've discovered something terrible," he began, his voice still a little strained. "The sound of the cicadas that is destroying this city is not a natural phenomenon. It has been manipulated by a ritual recorded on a vinyl we found."

The survivors listened in silence, their faces tense and attentive. Walker continued: "The caves north of Richmond—the same caves that have been rumored to be cursed for centuries—have a unique formation. They are made of limestone, a material that amplifies sound. The cicadas are drawn to those caves, and their chirping, which would normally just be annoying, has become unbearably loud because of this. But there's more: the ritual recorded on that vinyl has awakened something, causing the cicadas to enter an uncontrolled reproductive cycle that has led to this disaster."

Margaret's eyes widened in surprise and terror. "Then what can we do?" she asked, her voice trembling.

"We need to build a device," Walker explained. "A phase-inversion device that could cancel out the frequencies generated by the cicadas and stop this nightmare. But we need to build it quickly, and we'll need books, manuals to help us perfect the device. There might be what we need here in the library."

The survivors, shocked by Walker's words, began murmuring among themselves, trying to process what they had just heard—something straight out of a horror movie. Emily, who had previously discussed the book and the vinyl with Bet, stood up, her face resolute. "We'll find what we need, everyone. Each of us will do everything possible to help. We must stay united in this fight."

Walker, with an expression of gratitude, leaned back against the chair. Bet watched him, her heart heavy with the enormous responsibility that weighed on them, but she knew time was against them. There was still a spark of hope, a chance to save Richmond from the abyss it was descending into. She looked at her mother with a different expression, feeling for the first time what it meant to be responsible for someone, to remain strong and composed for others' sake. A powerful wave of emotion washed over her, and she finally understood her mother's coldness and forgave her.

As the group prepared to get to work, Walker briefly closed his eyes, trying to gather his strength. He knew that every minute was precious and that time was running out. But as long as there was a breath left in him, he would keep fighting.

And so, with the cicadas' chirping still echoing through the city, but safe within the solid walls of the library, the group began to brace themselves mentally for what lay ahead.

Chapter 10: The Calm Before the Storm

The Richmond library had become a fortress against the horror raging outside. The sound of the cicadas, which had previously been just an irritating background noise, had transformed into a full-blown sonic storm. It was as if the entire city had been wrapped in a constant, piercing scream, a relentless chirping that left no escape for anyone unlucky enough to be caught outside without protection. Attempting to leave the library would have been madness; anyone who did so without ear protection would either fall into insanity or, worse, die on the spot.

Inside, the group tried to maintain their calm and focus. Bet, James, Professor Walker, Margaret, Emily, and a few other survivors had gathered around a large wooden table. The atmosphere was heavy with tension, but there was also a growing sense of solidarity, a bond forming between them. It was as though, despite everything, they had found an anchor in each other.

Professor Walker was absorbed in reading books on applied sound physics and electronic engineering, desperately searching for a way to build the device that might save them. Next to him, Emily watched him attentively, gently passing the books he requested, never losing track of the discussion. Walker seemed incredibly focused, almost as if he were used to finding refuge in science during crises.

"Professor Walker," Emily asked, breaking the silence as she handed him an old, worn-covered book, "what led you to excel in such a particular field?"

The professor looked up from his notes, and his expression darkened for a moment, as if a cherished memory had touched him. He took a breath. "My wife," he began in a hoarse voice. "I lost her five years ago due to a heart complication. She was the center of my world, and when she passed, I threw myself into my work. Science... sound... became my refuge, my escape from the pain."

Emily looked at him with a tenderness she couldn't hide. "That must have been terrible."

Walker nodded, returning his gaze to the book in his hands, though his eyes seemed distant. "It was. For a long time, all I could do was work, hoping that somehow, I might find a way to fill the void she left in my life. But you know what I realized? You can't fill that void. You can only learn to live with it. And please, call me Walker."

Emily moved slightly closer, gently touching Walker's hand. "You're strong, Walker, and now you're using that strength to try to save all of us, this city."

Walker met Emily's gaze, and for a moment, the world outside seemed to quiet down, leaving them alone in that small corner of the library. "Thank you for what you do for us," he said, his voice warm and sincere. "You bring great strength to this group, even if you don't realize it."

Meanwhile, Bet and James sat on an old couch in a corner of the room, away from the main table. They had decided to take a moment to reflect on everything that was happening, but the real reason they had moved aside was to spend some time alone. Their bond, which had strengthened day by day, was now growing into something more.

"James," Bet began, her voice trembling as she nervously played with a strand of hair, "I never imagined I'd find myself in a situation like this, but I'm grateful that you're here with me."

James turned to her, his gaze full of affection and concern. "Me too, Bet. If there's one thing this madness has taught me, it's how important it is not to leave things unresolved. And between us..."

"There have been too many unresolved things for too long," Bet continued, finishing James's sentence as his languid eyes never stopped gazing at her.

Bet returned his gaze, her heart pounding harder. "You're right. I was so focused on running away from everything, trying to find my place in the world far from here, that I never realized what I was looking for had always been right in front of me."

James gently took her hand, intertwining his fingers with hers. "It doesn't matter where we go anymore, Bet. What matters is that we do it together."

James's words were like balm to Bet's soul, wrapping her in a sense of security she hadn't felt in a long time. Without thinking, she moved closer to him, resting her head on his shoulder. "I've always known there was something special between us, but I was afraid. Afraid of losing the little I had built if things didn't turn out the way I hoped."

James caressed her cheek with his free hand, tilting his head to look at her more closely. "We don't need to be afraid, Bet. Whatever happens, we'll face it together. I don't want to hide what I feel for you anymore... I've always loved you, deep down, and you know that."

James's words filled Bet's heart with warmth, and she realized that she, too, loved him, perhaps always had. "I don't want to live with regrets anymore."

Their faces slowly drew closer. James's lips, soft and waiting for this moment all his life, met hers. Bet's thoughts stopped in that instant. It was as if everything else had disappeared. It was a sweet kiss, full of unspoken emotions, a moment that seemed almost suspended in time.

James could smell the delicate scent of Bet's skin, his hand trembling slightly as he touched her. It wasn't until they pulled away, their hearts beating as one, that Bet realized how deep her feelings for James truly were. A long look passed between them, making time seem to stand still as they breathed in unison, their hearts pounding wildly.

In the next room, Emily handed another book to Professor Walker, their growing closeness becoming evident. Walker noticed a depth in her eyes, a quietness that reflected some of his own. He returned to leafing through the book but couldn't help thinking about what lay behind that calm facade.

"Emily," Walker began, trying to find the right words, "you must be very attached to this library.

It's not common for someone to dedicate so much time and passion to a place."

Emily smiled faintly, lowering her gaze to the books. "Books have always been a constant for me. They have an order, a stability that... the rest of the world sometimes lacks."

Walker nodded, feeling an affinity with what she was saying. He, too, had found refuge in his work after losing his wife. "I understand what you mean," he replied, his tone betraying subtle emotion. "After my wife died, science became my way of staying grounded. It was something I could count on, something I could understand."

Emily looked up, studying Walker's face carefully. "It's hard when you lose someone," she murmured, not wanting to invade his privacy but at the same time seeking a connection. "I lost someone too, in a way. Not... through death, but someone I thought would be by my side forever."

Walker remained silent for a moment, then asked, without pushing: "What happened?"

Emily hesitated but then decided to open up a little. "I was supposed to get married years ago, but when we found out I couldn't have children… and when he realized how attached I was to this place, he left. I shut down that part of myself and dedicated my days to this place. My safe haven."

Walker looked at her, feeling a pang of understanding. "I get it," he said, his voice low but full of empathy. "Sometimes, pain leads us to make choices that feel safe. I… buried myself in work to avoid feeling that emptiness. But over time, I realized work can't fill everything."

Emily nodded, recognizing that truth in her own experiences. "It's true," she admitted. "But maybe, amidst all this…" she said, not finishing the sentence. Walker gave her a look that communicated more than words could. "Maybe," he said with a soft, sweet smile, leaving the words hanging between them, charged with unspoken meaning.

As they returned to their books, both knew that moment had marked a change. No more needed to be said. For now, their priorities were clear: build the device, protect the people around them. But in their hearts, there was a new, timid acknowledgment that perhaps, after so long, they were no longer alone.

The silence that followed was broken only by the incessant chirping of the cicadas, now perhaps too much even for the old library. Bet pulled her hands away from James's and turned toward the windows, a worried expression on her face. "We need to find a way to stop this nightmare," she thought.

Having finished reading one of the books, Walker made a decision. He stood up and approached the group, with Emily following closely behind. "I think I've found a way to build and enhance the device," he said, glancing at Emily before continuing. "But we're going to need to work together, all of us."

Emily smiled at him. There was something beyond mere collaboration for a common goal. It was a deep connection, born from shared traumatic experiences and the discovery of an affinity they had both perhaps forgotten they could feel.

As the group gathered around the table to discuss the next steps, Bet and James exchanged one last look full of unspoken promises. They knew the time for sweet words was coming to an end and that soon they would have to face reality. But for now, they had found something precious, something worth fighting for.

Walker began explaining his plan as the sonic storm outside continued unabated. They knew time was against them, but they were ready to put everything they had into saving the city.

The battle was only beginning, but for the first time, they felt they had a chance to stop the sound of madness. And they wouldn't waste this one opportunity.

Chapter 11: The Device

At dawn, the streets of Richmond were filled with the relentless chirping of the cicadas, a constant, hammering sound that seemed intent on breaking the sanity of anyone exposed to it for too long. Inside the library, the group of survivors clung desperately to a single hope: a device that Walker and James had designed and were now assembling with the help of Emily and Bet.

The night had been a long, sleepless stretch. Margaret helped prepare something to refresh the group after their brief, disjointed naps.
Bet wasn't happy about not being able to help more than the twenty or so people who had taken refuge in the library, but she knew she couldn't have done more than she already had.

She thought about the people left outside: Mrs. Corinne, who had always given her a cookie when she was little and went to the bakery; the boy named Bob, who always teased her by riding his bike when they were children; the Mexican man who had opened a restaurant on the corner of Mulberry Street years ago; Annette, her college friend, who had just had a baby a few months ago; Susy, the mayor's assistant, who was always organizing charity events; and many other faces, some more familiar than others. Bet's heart tightened as she thought about the fate of those left outside.

While Bet coordinated the group, James and Walker were searching the library for something that could serve as a casing for the device. The library was full of dusty corners and forgotten rooms where cardboard boxes and old drawers lay unused for years. However, none of these items seemed sturdy enough or suitable to house the technical complexity of the device.

It was Emily who, almost by chance, found a solution. While rummaging through her belongings, she came across an old toolbox she used for small repairs around the library. "It's not much," she said, handing it to James and Walker, "but it might help."

The toolbox, well-worn and weathered, was perfect for their purpose. Inside were lightbulbs, nails, screws, and screwdrivers—tools that could come in handy during the device's construction. But what made the toolbox truly valuable were its compartments, ideal for organizing the various components of the device.

"This could be our salvation," James said, carefully examining the toolbox. The lower compartments could house the amplifiers, providing a low center of gravity for stability. The cables and modulators could be organized in the side compartments, easily connecting them to the laptop and amplifiers. Even the speakers could be mounted outside the toolbox, using adjustable arms to direct the sound without overly altering the appearance of the case.

James and Walker set to work with a clear vision: to build a device capable of canceling out the cicadas' chirping and playing the ritual extracted from the vinyl, all within a simple-looking wooden case containing advanced and complex technology.

"The counterphase of the cicadas' chirping! We need to carefully extract and filter it," Walker said as he worked on his laptop. "And the ritual recording—this is the key."

The laptop would serve as the control center of the device, sending signals to the other components through a long, shielded cable to ensure interference-free transmission.

Inside the toolbox, James and Walker precisely mounted a system of power amplifiers, essential for boosting the emitted signal. The amplifiers, powered by a well-hidden portable battery, would take the filtered signal from the laptop and transmit it through the connected speakers.

Holding four small speakers, James approached the worktable. "We can mount four speakers on the top of the toolbox, each fixed to an adjustable arm."

These arms would allow them to adjust the direction of each speaker to cover the entire surrounding area with near 360-degree precision. Despite the compact size, the speakers were powerful enough to ensure the sound would project everywhere, leaving no dead zones.

"Now, let's connect my laptop via the cable to the toolbox. It will manage the simultaneous emission of two frequencies: the counterphase, inverted by 180 degrees to cancel the cicadas' chirping, and the ritual, which should complete the process of neutralizing the dark power. Once the laptop transmits the signal to the amplifiers, it will be amplified and transmitted to the speakers to be emitted into the air." Walker's eyes were focused, his expression intent on his work. He knew the city's fate rested on this small contraption.

The toolbox/device, deceptively simple in appearance, was now a highly technical piece of equipment. Each component worked in synergy: the laptop, with the filtered frequencies, sent the signals to the amplifiers; the speakers mounted on the adjustable arms ensured the sound covered every possible direction, guaranteeing that the device's effect spread over a wide area.

"It won't be perfect," Walker admitted, tightening one last bolt, "but it should work."

When the device was finally assembled, it looked like a hybrid object—part ordinary toolbox, part complex electronic apparatus. Its portability was a huge advantage: once closed, the box could be easily transported, allowing them to move quickly without worrying about the components falling apart. It was an improvised solution, but effective.

The group gathered in the library's large entrance hall, once reserved for conferences and public readings, now transformed into an impromptu operations center. The atmosphere was thick with tension; every sound, every movement seemed amplified by the general anxiety. The dim light from the lamps cast uncertain shadows on the walls, accentuating the sense of oppression.

They knew the first test of the device would be crucial but also dangerous. Opening the library's doors meant exposing everyone to the deadly chirping, a risk they couldn't afford to take lightly.

"First of all, we need to get everyone out of here," Walker said, tightening the last bolts. "We can't risk anyone being hit by the chirping when we open the doors."

James nodded in agreement. "Anyone near the doors when we open them will be exposed to the sound, and we can't let that happen."

Emily coordinated moving the other survivors to a room deeper inside the library, away from the main entrance. People moved in silence, their terror evident in their eyes. Each one of them knew the risks they were taking, but they also knew they had no other choice. Bet held her mother's hand, trying to reassure her. The air was thick with tension as James and Walker prepared for the next step.

They approached the library's entrance, wearing the headphones they had used to get there—the same ones that had protected them from the devastating chirping as they moved through the city. The headphones were heavy, designed to block as much sound as possible, but even with them on, they knew the risk was still high.

"If something goes wrong, shut the door immediately," Walker told James as he prepared to unlock the entrance. "Even though the library was designed to muffle and dampen sound, with the doors open, we'll have serious problems keeping our minds clear."

Walker nodded, his face clearly tense as he checked that the headphones were securely in place. "We need to be quick and precise. We don't have room for error."

With a nod, Walker began unlocking the library's ancient doors—the same doors that had welcomed students, readers, and scholars for decades were now the barrier between life and death. As the doors opened, the devastating chirping poured into the library like a tidal wave, but the headphones dampened the sound enough for them to proceed.

James and Walker carefully moved the device just outside the entrance. Their hands trembled slightly, not because of uncertainty about their construction, but because of the awareness of the risk they were taking. If the device didn't work, there would be no way to stop that cursed and devastating sound.

"Now," James murmured, quickly connecting the cables to the speakers, positioning them strategically to cover as much area as possible.

Once they were sure the device was properly placed, they quickly reentered the library, closing the heavy doors behind them, which separated them from the deadly sound. Only then did they remove their headphones, exchanging a look of understanding. It was time for the truth.

With the device in place and extreme care taken to ensure the electrical cables weren't cut, the two cautiously approached the door, pressing their ears against the thick wood. Even with the protection of the library, the cicadas' chirping was still audible —a constant reminder of the danger surrounding them.

"We need to listen carefully," Walker whispered. "The chirping should decrease if the device is working properly."

James nodded, focusing on the sound that penetrated through the door. The chirping seemed to intensify for a moment, as if the cicadas had sensed the threat. Then, gradually, the sound began to change. The frequencies softened, oscillating between sharp and distorted tones.

"Is it working?" Bet asked, her voice filled with hope and fear, as she slowly approached from the other room.

"I think so," James replied, concentrating. "The sound is weakening…"

The effect became clear. The chirping lessened further, becoming a whisper, then a murmur, and finally… silence. A silence so deep it seemed unreal. For a moment, they remained motionless, unable to believe that the device had actually worked.

"It's working!" James murmured, smiling in disbelief. "God, it's really working!"

Walker moved to the monitors connected to the device, carefully observing the signals. His hands moved quickly over the controls, checking that everything was stable. "The signal is stable… it's working!"

As the group began to recover from the shock and tension with a glimmer of relief, Steven Harper, a survivor who had joined them only a few days earlier, started to lose his grip. Harper was a former mechanical engineer, a middle-aged man with graying hair and a face marked by despair. He had watched his life fall apart when chaos overwhelmed Richmond, taking his family with it, and now it seemed his despair had reached its breaking point.

"We can't stay here," Harper said, his voice trembling and his eyes wide with terror. "We can't keep hiding. This place is cursed—I need to get out of here!"

Emily tried to calm him, approaching slowly. "Steven, wait. We're still testing the device. We don't know exactly how it works or how long it will hold."

But Harper wasn't listening. His eyes were those of a man in full-blown panic, unable to think rationally. "There's no time! I have to leave. I need to find a car and get as far away as possible."

Before anyone could stop him, Harper rushed toward the library entrance, where the doors were still closed. James and Walker exchanged anxious glances as Harper approached.

"Don't do it, Harper!" James shouted, trying to stop him, but the man was already determined. In a reckless move, he grabbed the door handles and, ignoring the others' shouts, flung them open. The device was working, protecting those inside the library despite the doors being opened, but they still didn't know how effective it was or what problems they might encounter.

Harper ran outside, heading toward an abandoned car not far away. The group stood frozen for a moment, watching Harper's sprint, unsure of how to react. James called after him, but the man was already outside.

Harper ran toward the car, convinced he had found a way out. For a few moments, it seemed like the device was really working: the chirping had ceased, and everything around him was immersed in an unnatural silence. But as soon as he crossed about a hundred meters from the library, the unthinkable happened.

The cicadas' chirping suddenly returned, this time as a deafening scream in Harper's ears. He stopped dead in his tracks, clutching his head with his hands. A cry of pain escaped his lips, his ears began to bleed, and the pain was unbearable, sharp as a scalpel.

From their vantage point, Emily, James, and the others watched in horror as Harper fought against something invisible. He looked like he was about to collapse, his movements erratic and convulsive. The man bent forward, fell to the ground, and convulsed violently.

"Oh my God," Emily murmured, her heart freezing in her chest. Tears began streaming down her face, but she couldn't tear her eyes away from what was happening.

Harper desperately tried to get up, but every movement brought new waves of pain. His muscles contracted violently until he could no longer move. The chirping, now a hammering sound in his head, was killing him. His eyes dimmed as life left him.

James felt paralyzed, unable to look away from Harper's lifeless body.
"Close it, James, close the doors!" the professor shouted. James sprang into action, slamming the

heavy wooden door shut: "We've created a sort of invisible wall," he said in a low voice. "Beyond that point, the chirping comes back... and it kills."

"Yes," Walker said, "about a hundred meters—that's what separates us from death, and we've learned it the hard way."

Harper's death deeply shook the group. Not only for the brutality of how it had happened but also for the terror it instilled. If the device had such a precise limit, then they couldn't consider themselves safe, even just a few steps outside the library. Emily, visibly shaken, kept staring at the door as if she feared it would swing open again at any moment, bringing the deadly sound back inside.

"We can't go on like this," she said. "We don't know enough about the device... and Steven died because of that. We should have been more cautious..."

Bet nodded, feeling bewildered. They had tried to do everything as best as they could, but they had been caught off guard. Harper had acted in panic, endangering everyone else, and the device, which was supposed to protect them, had revealed its limits in the most brutal way.

"There's no time to mourn," Walker said, though his voice betrayed the tension. "We need to find a way to extend the device's effectiveness, to give us more coverage once we leave the library. If we don't, and we don't know the distance it covers, it could happen again."

Bet ran a hand through her hair, trying to pull herself together. "What can we do? The device has a limited range, and we can't move it too far from its power source."

James, his eyes fixed on the device that was still emitting its signal at full power, tried to think of a solution. "We need to boost the device's power or find a way to connect it to multiple power sources. And we need to do it fast."

The group retreated to the library's central hall to discuss ways to keep the device operational once it was moved to the cave, but there was a deathly silence. Harper's death had left a mark on all of them, those scenes so dramatic now clinging to their thoughts like the strongest of adhesives.

Despite still being disturbed by the events, Walker tried to remain calm. "One option is to use solar panels," he began, tracing his finger across a map of the area near the cave. "We could install them above the cave or in an open area, away from the cicadas' coverage. But there's an obvious problem: the cicadas."

James nodded, thinking over the proposal. "The cicadas are everywhere, and if they cover the solar panels, we won't have enough light to power the device. One way to avoid this is to place the panels far away from the cave, in a well-exposed area, and connect them with very long cables. But this would involve risks of energy dispersion and potential damage to the cables."

It was then that Emily, the librarian, spoke up with a determined tone, trying to hide the tremor in her voice. "I don't know if it will help, but the library has an old diesel generator. We've used it occasionally during blackouts or when there were municipal works on the high-voltage cables that cut the power. It hasn't been used much, but it should still work."

Walker turned to her, surprised by the revelation. "A diesel generator? How old is it? Could it really work?"

"It's old, but it's been well-maintained," Emily replied. "I had it serviced last year, around this time, and it hasn't been used since. It's old, but it's sturdy."

James seemed to regain some confidence. "If we can keep the generator running without interruptions, we might have a solution. It's not perfect, but it could work. We could take it with us, near the cave, and use it to power the device."

The old diesel generator was retrieved from the library's service room by Emily, and Walker immediately got to work ensuring it was in working condition. Despite its age, the generator seemed to be in good shape. It had a solid, built-to-last look, but there was still much to do.

"We need to know exactly how much fuel we'll need. We can't afford to run out in the middle of the operation," the professor said, holding a worn notebook to do some calculations.

"How much does it consume?" James asked, watching Walker carefully.

"If it works as expected, it should consume about 0.75 liters of fuel per hour under load. With a full tank, we have about 20 liters. That means we can run it for about 26-27 hours, maybe 30 if we optimize the load," Walker replied.

James thought for a moment, then nodded. "That should be enough to keep the device running for as long as we need to reach the cave, lower it inside, and use the cave's own amplification—amplifying the cicadas to counter the sound and neutralize it effectively. But we'll need to be ready to refuel if necessary."

Walker continued with his calculations, noting every detail. "We can't afford mistakes. Every liter of fuel must be used efficiently. If we stop for any reason, we'll have to start all over again, and it could be too late."

With the calculations done and the plan laid out, the group prepared to transport the generator and the device to the cave. It wasn't an easy task, but they were determined to make it work. The generator was loaded onto an old cart found in the library and hitched to Walker's old station wagon, with extra fuel divided into cans to make transportation easier.

"We need to be quick and precise," Walker said, giving the final instructions. "We can't afford to waste time. Every minute is precious."

James nodded. "We can position the generator near the cave, but not too close to avoid exposure to the cicadas. We'll use long cables to connect it to the device inside the cave. That way, we can keep the generator protected and away from any issues caused by the cicadas."

In the library's central hall, the tension was palpable. James addressed the group. "We need to be clear: we can't take everyone to the cave. It's too dangerous, and we can't risk losing more people. But we need those who know what to do."

Emily, her voice steady but with a slight tremble, added: "The cave is an unknown. We don't know what to expect out there, and if something goes wrong, we need to be ready for anything."

A murmur rose among the survivors. Lucas, a man with graying hair and a scar running across his cheek, tried to object, his voice breaking with emotion: "How can we help? If something goes wrong..."

Walker responded calmly but firmly: "We need to be rational. James built the device; he's the only one who can fix any technical problems. I have the scientific and engineering knowledge needed to handle any issues. Bet has been on the front lines since the beginning; she knows how to handle danger and intervene if necessary, and Emily knows the maps and the history of the area. She's our best guide."

Bet, who had remained silent until that moment, felt the weight of responsibility growing inside her. Finally, she raised her head, trying to control the emotion in her voice: "I know it's not fair, but it's not about fairness now. It's about survival. We have to make sure that if something goes wrong, someone stays behind to continue the fight, to take care of each other, and to tell what happened. We can't afford to have anyone else risk their lives."

A heavy silence followed those words. The atmosphere grew even more tense when Margaret, Bet's mother, spoke up. Her face was marked by worry, and her eyes were filled with deep concern.

"Bet, you can't do this..." Margaret's voice was broken, almost a painful whisper. Heavy tears ran down her cheeks. Bet had never seen her mother cry like this. "I can't lose you too, not after everything we've been through."

Bet turned to her mother, feeling the pain in her voice like a stab to the heart. "Mom... I know, but there's nothing else to do, and I... I have to be there."

Margaret stared at her, her tears now uncontrollable. "You've already done so much, Bet. You've been so strong... but I'm your mother. I can't let you go," she added in a stern voice.

Bet approached her, taking her hands in hers, her words soft but resolute. "Mom, if we don't go, there won't be anything left to fight for. I have to do this for you, for Dad, for all of us. And I will come back, I promise."

Margaret lowered her gaze, unable to speak for a moment, then slowly nodded, trying to find the strength to let her daughter go. "Come back to me, Bet. Come back..." Bet squeezed her hands tightly, trying to convey all her determination. "I will come back, Mom. I promise," she said, hugging her tightly. "I came back for you, and I'll come back again."

Emily, watching the scene with a mix of respect and concern, stepped in to break the emotional moment. "We won't be alone, Margaret. We'll do everything we can to come back together."

Bet, still beside her mother, responded with a small, sad but determined smile: "We'll do our best, I promise. But now we have to go. It's the only way to save Richmond, to save all of us." Walker, with calm determination, concluded: "We're ready! Let's go."

The group exchanged a look of understanding. It was a moment of great responsibility but also of unity. The four knew that the mission's success—and perhaps Richmond's—depended on them. Without further words, they prepared to leave, knowing that each step could be their last, but determined not to fail.

With the generator fueled and the device ready to be transported, maps and a few books, the group set out to face the cave. Despite the uncertainties and dangers, they knew this was the final step in stopping the madness that had gripped Richmond.

As the sound of the generator filled the air, almost drowning out the distant chirping of the cicadas, Walker loaded the car with tools and cables that might come in handy, while James quickly connected the device directly to the generator to provide that crucial 100 meters of protection around them and the vehicle. For the first time, the group felt a bit safer, but they knew the real test would come once they reached the cave.

It was almost dusk, and they set off toward their destiny, knowing that the city's fate rested on them and the steady hum of an old diesel generator that could not afford to fail.

Chapter 12: Through the City

The city of Richmond, once teeming with life, now lay under a veil of death and desolation. The oppressive heat that had gripped the city since the first signs of the cicada outbreak continued to suffocate everything, like a suffocating shroud that allowed no reprieve. The setting sun, hidden behind a blanket of dense, murky clouds, still emitted an unbearable heat, transforming the air into yet another invisible enemy. The streets were barren and silent, as if the entire city were holding its breath.

Walker's old station wagon moved slowly along the deserted streets, towing the cart with the generator and the device. The engine roared dully, almost fatigued, as if it too felt the weight of the heat and the tension pressing down on all of them. The device emitted a constant hum, a monotonous yet reassuring sound that repelled the cicadas' deafening drone, creating a protective bubble of about one hundred meters around them. But that silence, though life-saving, carried a sense of foreboding that pierced their skin, a premonition of what awaited them beyond.

Inside the vehicle, the heat was unbearable. Air conditioning was a luxury they had sacrificed to save fuel, leaving them in a stifling environment where sweat poured from their faces and ears, shielded by protective headphones. The acrid smell of overheated metal and sweat permeated the air, mixing with the stench of something rotten that seemed to seep from the city's depths.

James, sitting next to Walker, watched the monitor connected to the device closely, ensuring everything was in order and that the device was emitting the counter-phase frequency. Occasionally, his hand nervously gripped the edge of the console, as beads of sweat slid down his forehead. "So far, so good," he muttered, trying to reassure himself and the others. "The device is keeping us safe."

Walker nodded, gripping the steering wheel with sweaty hands covered in a thin layer of dust. His eyes scanned the road ahead, each shadow, each reflection a potential threat. The stifling heat made it difficult to focus, and the humidity in the air made their skin feel sticky and irritated. "We just have to hope the generator doesn't fail us," he said tensely. "If it stops, we're done for."

In the back, Bet tried to shake off the overwhelming feeling of suffocation engulfing her. Sweat drenched her clothes, and the heat inside the car seemed to amplify her anxiety. "We just have to keep moving," she said, more to herself than to the others. "We can't stop."

Emily, sitting next to Bet, watched the road through the dirty window. The sky over Richmond was darkened by thick clouds and the approaching night. "The city is dying," she whispered sadly. "There's nothing left here."

As they continued, the urban landscape around them seemed to close in, almost swallowing them in a grip of darkness. The streets became narrower and more claustrophobic, with crumbling buildings looming like ghosts from a past era. The scorching asphalt exuded a smell of bitumen that mixed with the hot, sticky air, making every breath a struggle.

The unnatural silence, interrupted only by the device's hum and the engine's growl, made the journey even more surreal. Richmond now seemed to be holding its breath, as if waiting for something terrible to happen.

Suddenly, James spotted something outside the window. "Walker, look over there!" he exclaimed, pointing to a distant spot. Just outside the protective bubble, a group of cicadas seemed to have gathered in a pulsating mass, their deformed, iridescent bodies reflecting the dim light of the day. "They seem attracted to the device," he continued, worried.

Walker sped up slightly, trying to avoid contact with the living wall. "Don't stop," Emily said, her voice strained with fear.

Suddenly, a terrifying blow struck the car as they passed by the group. Walker momentarily lost control of the car, struggling to regain it in a split second of fear. "What's happening?!" Emily screamed in panic.

One of the larger cicadas had detached from the swarm and slammed violently into the passenger-side window. The glass cracked under the impact but didn't shatter. The cicada slid off, leaving a slimy trail on the surface.

"Damn it!" Bet yelled, her heart pounding in her chest. "Don't slow down, Walker!"

Walker kept his foot on the pedal, his hands gripping the steering wheel so tightly his knuckles turned white. James watched the generator through the rearview mirror, worried that the impact might have caused some damage. They kept driving, but the tension inside the vehicle was palpable.

As the station wagon continued to navigate Richmond's empty, dark streets, the oppressive heat gave no respite. The air inside the vehicle was thick and saturated. The monotonous hum of the device, which had so far protected them from the cicadas' screeching, seemed like the only barrier between them and madness.

Suddenly, James noticed a flicker on the device's monitor. "Walker, slow down a bit," he said, trying not to sound panicked.

Walker obeyed, easing the car's speed as the tension inside grew. "The device is still working, right?"

James leaned toward the device, checking the connections and readings. But before he could answer, the reassuring hum abruptly cut off, replaced by an eerie silence. A moment later, the cicadas' screech erupted all around them, filling the air with a sharp, piercing sound, a sound capable of driving anyone exposed to it mad.

"What the hell is going on!" Walker shouted, accelerating as the cicadas' screech seemed to close in on them like a deadly grip.

Immediately, all four of them were overwhelmed by a wave of pain. Their ears throbbed under the headphones, and the sound, piercing their brains despite the protection, became so intense that they screamed involuntarily. James doubled over, teeth clenched, as the world around him warped into a vortex of pain and devastating sound.

"James, do something!" Walker yelled, though his words were lost in the chaotic noise. Every second brought them closer to madness, and their sanity

began to slip away, dragged down by the deafening roar.

With trembling hands and a sound that seemed bent on annihilating them, James desperately searched for the cause of the malfunction. His vision blurred with pain, and for a moment, he feared he wouldn't make it—that the cicadas' screech would be the last sound he'd ever hear. Then, with one last effort, his fingers found a loose cable, dislodged from its socket by the vibrations of the journey.

"I've almost got it!" he shouted, but his voice was a faint echo in his foggy mind. With a quick, desperate motion, he pushed the cable back into place, finally hearing the reassuring click.

For a moment, it seemed like nothing had changed. The cicadas' screech still reverberated in their heads, now unbearable. Then, the hum of the device slowly returned, growing until it repelled the infernal sound, restoring the much-needed protection.

The invisible, deadly sound was pushed back once again, and the screech faded away until it vanished completely. But inside the car, the damage had already been done. They were all still twisted in pain, struggling to recover. Walker, pale-faced, gripped the steering wheel tightly, desperately trying to stay focused.

"Christ..." James muttered, slumping back against the seat. "Not even the headphones will protect us now; the sound is so strong it's breaking through every barrier!" The pain still throbbed in his head, but the regained silence was almost deafening.

Bet wiped her sweaty forehead with a trembling hand. "We were one step... away from losing ourselves, or worse, dying," she whispered, trying to catch her breath.

Emily, still shaking, looked out the window, as if the landscape could help her find some sense of stability. "I thought I was going insane... I couldn't think..."

Walker, breathing heavily, forced himself to speak. "We can't let that happen again. We were too close... too close."

Walker kept driving, his gaze fixed on the road, with a calm that seemed to come from nowhere. He had no choice—panic wouldn't help. The sound had left behind a sense of emptiness, as if it had stolen a piece of their souls. But they knew they couldn't slow down.

"James," Walker said, his voice still trembling, "is the device holding?"

James checked the connections again, making sure everything was in place. "Yeah... it should hold. But we need to move now, before it happens again!"

The journey continued, but the incident had left its mark. Every small noise, every vibration made them jump, fearing that their protection might collapse again. The oppressive heat and the heavy air didn't help, heightening the sense of claustrophobia and vulnerability.

The silence inside the vehicle had become suffocating, broken only by the monotonous hum of the device. They were approaching the hills that would lead them to the cave, following Emily's directions despite the fear knotting her stomach and the lingering pain in her ears, a constant reminder of how close they had come to the end.

As they pressed on, they came upon a bridge spanning a small river that cut through the city. A portion of the cicadas seemed to have gathered there, perhaps drawn by the moisture or the presence of the water. Walker instinctively slowed down, trying to figure out how to cross that living barrier. "We can't stop," James exclaimed.

"We have no choice," Walker replied. "If we try to cross, we could be overwhelmed."

As they debated, a series of sinister noises cut through the air. It sounded like something was moving beneath the wooden bridge, a sound of scratching and scraping that sent a shiver down everyone's spine.

"What the hell is that?" Bet asked, her face filled with horror.

Suddenly, a wave of cicadas surged from the underbrush near the bridge, like a horde of infernal creatures, swarming toward the car. The deafening screech of their wings seemed to challenge the protective bubble created by the device. The creatures hurled themselves against the invisible barrier, repelled at the last moment, writhing and dying on the ground only to be replaced by others.

"Walker, go!" Emily screamed, now completely panicked.

Walker didn't need to be told twice. With a sharp press on the accelerator, the station wagon lunged onto the bridge. The cicadas slammed into the vehicle and the generator from all sides, creating a sound like rain of claws on metal. The generator behind them barely stayed on, struggling to maintain its power but managing to propel the car forward through the nightmarish scene.

James looked back, his breath short, as the cart carrying the generator swayed dangerously from side to side. Every second felt like a fight against time and madness.

"We made it!" Bet exclaimed, her heart pounding, as they crossed the bridge, leaving the swarm of cicadas behind them. They kept driving, but the landscape changed rapidly. The roads grew narrower, more uneven, and the vegetation thickened as they neared the hills marking the beginning of the cave's area.

The night air was scorching, almost unbreathable, and every breath carried the pungent smell of hot earth and decaying foliage. Then they saw it: a scene straight out of a nightmare.

The hills and the area around the cave were completely covered in cicadas. Hundreds of thousands, perhaps millions, moved incessantly, creating a dark, undulating sea that covered every surface. The cicadas crawled over one another, pushing forward, all drawn to a dark point at the heart of the cave.

Emily stared at the scene in terror, her eyes wide. "It's worse than we imagined." Walker stopped the car at a safe distance, staring in horror at the sight before them. "How the hell are we going to get the device in there?" he asked, more to himself than to the others.

James stared at the cave, feeling the weight of the situation pressing down on his shoulders. "We have to find a way," he said with determination. "We didn't come this far to give up now."

Bet looked out into the darkness of the night, her heart pounding in her chest. The sight of the cicadas, a living wall blocking their path, was more terrifying than any nightmare. She had never imagined returning to Richmond and finding herself in such a surreal situation, nor facing death. But deep down, she knew she had to do it—for her mother, and for all the people who still had hope. She knew the real nightmare had just begun, but she had to put an end to everything that had caused her father's death. She had to do it. Especially for him.

Chapter 13: The Secret of the Cave

Walker's station wagon came to a stop just a few meters from the cave entrance. The engine, still growling, finally died down, leaving only the faint chirping of the cicadas, muffled by the device's sound wave. The group was tense, acutely aware that every minute lost increased the risk. The oppressive heat emanating from the surrounding rocks made every breath labored, while the dark sky above them warned of a night that might be their last.

"Before we go in, we need to make sure the cables are long enough to take the device inside the cave," Walker said, his gaze fixed on the darkness awaiting them. "And we need to refuel the generator."

James nodded, already pulling out the flashlights they would need inside the cave, along with the cables from the back of the vehicle. "We can't afford to run out of power in there," he said, his voice edged with concern. "If the device shuts off, even for a moment, we're finished."

As the others prepared the equipment, James, firmly securing his headphones on his head, approached the diesel generator with a fuel canister. With precise, calculated movements, he unscrewed the tank cap and began to pour the fuel. His hands trembled slightly, not from the weight of the canister, but from the awareness of the danger they were in.

Walker approached James, eyeing the cicada-covered cave entrance. "We've got about 25 hours of power once you refill the generator." James nodded, sealing the tank. "Yes, that should be enough time, but we need to move fast. We can't afford any delays."

With the generator refueled and the cables checked, the group prepared to enter. The device emitted its reassuring hum, but everyone knew they were standing on the edge of disaster. Every move had to be perfectly coordinated.

Emily watched the cicadas crawling over the cave entrance, their black, iridescent forms shifting in the flashlight beams. "There's no other way but through," she murmured, her voice thin and filled with dread.

With the device at full power, the group began to slowly move toward the cave. The concentrated sound created a narrow path between the cicadas, pushing them back just enough to allow passage. Each step was a test of nerves, with the constant risk that the sound barrier might fail.

"Watch the cables," Walker warned. "If we trip or tug them too hard, they could disconnect or even break, and we'd be dead in an instant!"

The cicadas, though repelled, seemed to follow their every move, ready to close the gap behind them.

Inside the cave, an eerie silence reigned, broken only by the labored breathing and the steady hum of the device. The cave was damp and cold, a sharp contrast to the heat outside, but the device seemed to keep the cicadas' drone at bay. The walls, illuminated by their flashlights, revealed what appeared to be ancient symbols etched into the stone.

Emily moved closer to examine them, fascinated by their complexity. "These symbols... they look Zapotec, an ancient civilization from around 500-600 B.C. in the Valley of Oaxaca, Mexico!" she said, gently tracing the carvings with her fingers. "It's as if whoever carved these knew their writing system very well."

Frowning, Walker approached the cave walls. "Zapotec? Here? Thousands of miles from Mexico? I didn't think their influence reached this far."

Bet, cautiously moving closer, observed the shape of a large monolith in the center of the cave. "It's not just that... look at how well-preserved this stone is. These symbols seem ancient, but they're intact. It doesn't make sense."

Intrigued, James approached the monolith to examine it more closely. "Wait a second..." he murmured, placing his hand on the smooth, cold surface. The moment his hand made contact with the monolith, a powerful vibration surged through his arm, causing him to jolt back. "Whoa!" he exclaimed, pulling his hand away. "This thing...

it's vibrating! But it's not just an ordinary vibration, it's like… it's resonating with the cicadas."

Emily nodded, her gaze fixed on the monolith. "Yes, that makes sense. The cicadas' drone is so intense that it's amplifying the vibrations of this natural tuning fork. It's as if, by resonating with the cicadas' frequency, it's amplifying it. That's why it seems like the sound never ends. This cave acts like a giant resonating chamber. But here, it talks about a ritual… I can't fully understand it yet. It probably explains how to use the ritual frequency we found on the vinyl. There are two intertwining waves."

Walker crouched to get a better look at the base of the monolith. "Yes, just as we suspected, but if we get it wrong, it could amplify the sound even more and destroy us."

James crouched next to the stone, examining it from every angle, and found small holes at the base, similar to those used in modern structures for connecting electrical cables. "These holes…" he said, running his fingers over them, "we can use them to connect the device. If it works, the cave itself will become a resonating chamber, and it could fix everything. But... it's risky."

Bet, her expression worried, stared at the stone, aware of the imminent danger. "How can you be sure? What if we fail? It could be the end!"

James shook his head. "I'm not sure, but something tells me it might work. We don't have much choice unless you're willing to take the risk."

The three exchanged determined looks, knowing that James understood what he was talking about. Bet trusted him, and deep down, she felt she had no choice but to rely on fate. After all, fate had brought her back to her great love, and deep in her heart, she felt there was still hope.

Taking a deep breath, James nodded at the group's consent. He began connecting the device's cables to the monolith, sweat dripping down his forehead as he felt the weight of the responsibility he had never experienced before. The hum of the device deepened and intensified as the energy flowed through the cables. Suddenly, the vibration of the monolith increased exponentially, and the cave began to shake violently.

The walls inside shifted, and pieces of stalactites started falling from the ceiling. Suddenly, one of the stalactites broke loose from the cave's height, hitting Emily on the shoulder. She fell to the ground with a cry. Blood began to flow profusely from the wound, staining the floor with dust and debris. "Emily! Hold on!" Bet shouted, running to her, trying to stop the bleeding as best as she could.

As the cave continued to tremble, one of the cables connected to the monolith suddenly disconnected due to the intense vibration, generating a devastating sonic boom. The entire cave filled with an overwhelming roar, as if a bomb had exploded from within. A flash of blinding light illuminated the cave, turning the environment white and oppressive. For a moment, it felt as if time had stopped.

James, Walker, and Bet were thrown back, instinctively covering their eyes. A piercing hum settled in their heads, and the world around them seemed to fade. They were completely deaf, unable to hear anything but a sharp, persistent sound. Their senses seemed to vanish, as if reality itself had been put on pause.

For several agonizing minutes, none of them could hear or see anything. The monolith had stopped vibrating, and the device's hum had completely ceased.

James was the first to slowly regain his senses, struggling to his feet. His head spun, and his ears throbbed painfully, even through the headphones. The device was off. The monolith appeared dead, motionless. There was no longer any sound of cicadas.

He looked around, noticing that Walker and Bet were slowly getting up from the ground, still dazed. The silence was deafening, unnatural, as if the entire world had ceased to exist. The only sound they could hear in the distance was the generator outside the cave, still running.

Bet approached Emily, who was still lying on the ground, injured and dazed from the blow. "Emily... hang in there. We'll get you out of here."

Walker got up, confused, his ears still ringing and his eyes sore from the sudden light. "What happened? Why... is everything off?"

James, still in shock, tried to piece things together. "I don't know... it looks like the monolith shut down... along with the device. It's as if the connection overloaded everything."

Bet looked toward the cave entrance. "And the cicadas? I can't hear them anymore." The silence, broken only by the distant hum of the generator, felt surreal. After months of incessant chirping, with nights and days tormented by the cicadas' drone, the emptiness was oppressive, unnatural, almost surreal.

James, cautiously, approached the monolith, which was now cold and still. He carefully examined the cables, trying to figure out what could have caused the explosion. "I think the monolith... adapted to the new frequency. The chirping has been... canceled, we don't hear anything anymore," he said, lifting one of his headphones slightly from his right ear.

But Walker, staring at the now-dead device, was worried about something else. "We don't know if this effect is temporary—they could start chirping again at any moment!"

James shook his head, uncertain. "I don't know, but for now… it seems to be working."

Bet nodded, helping Emily to her feet. "We need to get out of here now. Emily's lost too much blood, we can't stay."

The group slowly made their way toward the cave entrance, still disoriented from the sonic boom that had hit them. Bet held tightly to Emily, whose face was pale from the blood loss. James and Walker walked ahead, still shaken, trying to orient themselves in the eerie silence that now surrounded them.

When the sunlight finally began filtering through the entrance, their steps slowed. What they saw outside froze them in place.

Hundreds of thousands of dead cicadas covered the ground before them, piled into a dense, oppressive carpet. The fragile bodies of the insects stretched

for hundreds of meters, creating an endless black-green shroud. The broken wings of the cicadas faintly reflected the sunlight, and their rigid shells were everywhere, forming a macabre landscape.

Bet stood still for a moment, her eyes wide. "My God..." she murmured, almost unable to believe what she was seeing. "They're all dead."

Every step they took produced a disturbing sound, a dull crackle, like the crunch of dry bread underfoot, as their shoes sank slightly into the lifeless bodies of the cicadas. James moved slowly, his gaze fixed on the sea of death. The ground beneath his feet seemed to give way, crumbling under the pressure of their steps, and that rhythmic sound, almost unbearable, echoed in their minds.

Walker stared blankly at the scene, still dazed by the events that had just occurred. "It's as if everything shut down in an instant," he said quietly. "I can't believe they're... all dead."

The air around them was thick and hot, and a faint odor of decomposition began to mingle with the sweat and dust. The incessant chirping that had haunted them for days, weeks, had completely vanished. The silence was almost deafening.

Emily, barely able to stand, lifted her gaze to take in the desolate scene. Even in her semi-conscious state, she realized that the nightmare that had plagued them had come to a halt. "I don't hear... anything," she whispered weakly, her head resting on Bet's shoulder.

The only sound they could perceive, aside from the crackling of the cicadas beneath their feet, was the distant hum of the diesel generator outside the cave, still running, a mechanical echo in that sea of death and silence.

James paused for a moment, staring at the immense cicada death in the night. The carpet of death stretched to the horizon, with no apparent end. "Is it really over?" he whispered, almost afraid to speak too loudly and shatter the fragile balance.

Bet nodded slowly, still in disbelief. "It seems... it seems like it is."

As they made their way toward the exit, each step became slower, as if the disturbing sensation of walking on those fragile bodies was holding them back mentally and physically. Every step that sank into the dead cicadas produced a sound—crack, crack—amplifying the horror of the sight.

When they finally reached the generator, now exhausted and weighed down by everything they had witnessed, they stopped. The only sound left was the steady hum of the generator, their only signal that the outside world was still functioning, despite the horror they had just left behind.

James turned one last time toward the cave entrance and finally shut off the generator, watching the surreal scene of dead cicadas filling every visible space. The air was still, as if time itself had stopped along with the cicadas' chirping. That silence, so sudden and final, was a sign that the battle was over. But none of them could feel fully relieved. What they had experienced had shaken them to the core, and they had no idea what they would find beyond the barrier of cicadas.

Chapter 14: The Return to the City

The first light of dawn began to break through the gray sky as James, driving the old station wagon, slowed down along the road leading back to Richmond. The surreal silence surrounding them was oppressive, almost more unsettling than the incessant chirping of the cicadas. Only the hum of the engine could be heard, a sound that seemed out of place in the motionless world around them. There was no trace of life: no birds chirping, no other sounds. It was as if the entire city had been swallowed by a void of silence.

Sitting next to James, Bet struggled to push away thoughts of what they had just left behind. The madness they had lived through, the chirping that had threatened to tear their sanity apart, was finally over. But the air was still thick with fear. The absence of any animal sounds made everything feel unnatural. Every now and then, she glanced at the back seat, where Emily, visibly weakened, was trying to recover from the searing pain in her shoulder. Walker, sitting beside her, watched with concern, ready to help if needed.

"We're not alone," Walker muttered, breaking the silence. He pointed ahead to the main road of the city.

Bet looked up and noticed a few figures moving slowly along the sidewalk. Survivors. Men and women, marked by the nightmare they had endured, but who had managed to hold on. Some shuffled hesitantly, their hands still clutching their ears as if the cicadas' chirping still echoed in their minds. Others glanced around, frightened, unsure whether to trust the silence that now enveloped them.

James slowed the car even more as Walker opened the door to get out. "We need to talk to them," he said, without hesitation. "They need to know it's over."

"Some didn't make it," Bet murmured, watching as a figure dragged itself along the side of the road. The man moved stiffly, his motions jerky and disjointed, his eyes empty, like an abandoned puppet. He was one of those who hadn't been able to come back. Many minds had been shattered by the sound. Even now, with the chirping gone, they were not free.

"There's nothing we can do for them," James said tensely. "Focus on those who can be saved."

Walker approached a small group of people who were wandering aimlessly. "It's over!" he shouted, trying to catch their attention. "The cicadas' sound has stopped. Gather at the library; you'll be safe there."

The people stopped, some incredulous, others with exhaustion etched into their faces. A woman with disheveled hair and a dazed look stepped forward, clutching a child tightly. "Is it really over?" she asked in a trembling voice, her eyes filled with hope but also terror.

Bet nodded and walked toward her. "Yes, it's over. But we need to stay together. Come with us to the library, my mother and others are waiting for us there."

Gradually, the news began to spread. More survivors emerged from their homes, still cautious, unsure if it was truly safe. The car resumed its slow journey through Richmond's streets, with Walker and Bet stepping out at every block to speak with those they encountered, trying to gather everyone at the library. Some followed immediately, while others remained hesitant, too frightened or too broken by the madness to move.

As they passed through the city's central square, Bet couldn't help but notice how life had vanished. There was no sound, no sign of the usual activity that once defined the place. It was as if the city itself was holding its breath, still paralyzed by the terror that had gripped it.

"There will be time to mourn the dead," James said as he stopped the car in front of the library. "For now, we need to focus on those who survived."

The library doors were wide open, and on the threshold stood Margaret, Bet's mother, anxiously awaiting the group's return. When she saw Bet step out of the car, her face lit up, and without hesitation, she ran toward her.

"Bet!" Margaret cried, her voice breaking with emotion. Her arms opened wide, and she embraced

her tightly as soon as she was close. "We stopped hearing the chirping, we knew you had done it!"

"Mom!" Bet replied, finally feeling the weight of the past few days melt away in that embrace. She felt like a child again in her mother's arms, and though the terror hadn't completely disappeared, she could feel the warmth, and gratitude began to fill her heart. "It seems so," she said, exhaling deeply, releasing all the tension.

Margaret held her even tighter, almost as if she feared her daughter might vanish. "You don't know how much I prayed for this moment," she whispered, her voice trembling. "We're safe, but look around."

Bet pulled back slightly, looking into her mother's eyes. There was concern in the face, worn by years and stress. "What do you mean?" she asked, feeling the knot in her stomach tighten again.

"The city has changed," Margaret said softly. "Something has broken, Bet. The sound is gone, but the people... some of them will never be the same again."

Bet lowered her gaze, feeling the weight of her mother's words. "I know. I've seen it." She turned toward the group of survivors who were beginning to gather inside the library, while others continued to arrive. "But we have to do whatever we can to help those who can still be saved. Emily is hurt; we need to help her!"

Margaret nodded slowly as she accompanied Bet inside the library, followed by James, Walker, and Emily. Bet glanced one last time at the city. The streets were empty, the silence still oppressive, and the shadows of those who hadn't made it lingered like lost souls. Even though the sound had ceased, Richmond would never be the same.

Inside the library, the silence was broken only by the slow shuffle of the survivors, who gathered one by one in the large reading room. Some leaned against the walls, while others found refuge in the old upholstered chairs, exhausted, dazed, but alive. The sun, now rising high in the sky, filtered through the large windows, illuminating the book-covered walls, making the place feel like a sacred sanctuary, a bubble of peace in the midst of the chaos that had overwhelmed Richmond.

Margaret hurried to the emergency kit and returned, trying to dress Emily's wound as she writhed in pain. Bet searched for painkillers. "Take this," she said, handing her water and the medicine. "You'll feel better soon; the wound isn't too deep." Emily nodded, her face showing deep gratitude.

James and Walker moved to the center of the room. The group of survivors, their faces marked by anguish, watched them in anticipation. They wanted to know. They wanted to understand.

James cleared his throat, visibly tense. "I know you're all confused, scared," he began, his voice a bit hoarse. "But we're here, and that's what matters." He paused, searching for the right words. "Richmond has been through something none of us could have predicted... The cicadas' sound that tormented us wasn't natural."

The survivors' eyes widened, and the silence in the room grew heavier. James continued, his dark gaze meeting each face he saw. "I don't know where it came from or why it happened here, but that sound... it was capable of breaking our minds.

We've seen it with our own eyes. Some of you have lost loved ones, others have seen friends or neighbors succumb to a madness we couldn't stop."

An uneasy murmur rippled through the crowd. Margaret watched closely, holding Bet's hand. It was clear that each person was reliving those moments, those flashes of pure terror.

Walker stepped forward. "But we found a way to stop it," he said firmly, trying to maintain calm. "We managed to shut down the source of the sound. It was like breaking an invisible chain that was strangling the city. The sound, thank God, is gone. We don't yet know what the consequences of this action will be, but for now, we are safe. From what we've seen, all the cicadas are dead."

Relief was palpable. Some of the survivors began to breathe more deeply, as if only now realizing they could finally let go of the terror they had held onto for days.

"We don't know if this nightmare will return," Walker continued, looking at each face seriously.

"But for now, we've broken the chain, and we can find some peace."

A heavy silence followed his words, as if no one dared to believe it just yet. Margaret stood up, with a strength she hadn't felt in a long time, her eyes brimming with tears of hope. "Here, in the library, you'll be safe," she said, her voice firm yet gentle. "Take the time to rest, to regain your strength. Then, when you feel ready, you can return to your homes. Richmond is still here, and so are we." She turned to Bet with a meaningful look.

Bet looked around, observing the people clinging to each other, finding comfort in familiar faces and small gestures of reassurance. Some hugged, others held hands, while a gentle warmth began to fill the cold, quiet air of the library. It wasn't the end of the pain, but it was a beginning. A sign that, despite everything, there was still hope.

Slowly, the people began to relax. Some leaned against the bookshelves, closed their eyes, and let themselves drift into a deep sleep. Others sat quietly, watching the sunlight stream through the windows, as if just being alive was already a miracle.

Bet, standing next to her mother, watched the scene with a mix of relief and sadness. She knew Richmond would never be the same, that many lives had been shattered. But this moment, in this library that now seemed so welcoming, was a small step toward healing.

James approached Bet, looking at her with eyes that revealed his exhaustion. "We did it, Bet," he whispered, holding her tightly. "We did it."

Bet looked at him with a tired smile, but full of affection and gratitude. "Yes. We did it."

The sun slowly moved, its warmth enveloping everyone inside, like a cloak protecting them from the devastation. Slowly, without haste, people began to wake from their stupor, ready to return to their homes. It was a cautious return, but the cicadas' sound was now a distant memory, and with it, the horror that had engulfed the city.

As the last people left the library, Bet stood with James, Walker, and Margaret. She watched the small group disperse slowly, some holding hands, others walking alone. They knew the road back to normality would be long, but now they had a starting point.

"And now?" James asked, smiling at Bet with a tired grin.

Bet turned to her mother, then to Walker, and finally to the sun as it began to illuminate Richmond. "Now we live, every day is a gift. I realized that while we were in the cave. I had been wallowing and hiding for too long after my wife's death, but the line between life and death is so thin that all we have left to do is live our best lives," she said, a newfound determination in her eyes. "Protecting and loving everything we can." She glanced tenderly at Emily.

Chapter 15: Among the Shadows of Desire

Bet made sure that all the survivors in the library were well. The atmosphere, though still heavy with tension and exhaustion, seemed to lighten now that the danger had passed. The faces, marked by terror and fatigue, were slowly starting to recover. Some whispered softly, others tried to comfort each other. Every now and then, a murmur of hope mixed with the rustling of books and the faint sound of footsteps on the wooden floors.

She approached her mother, who had remained calm and composed despite the chaos of the last few hours. Margaret, with a loving yet determined look, watched her as she made her way through the crowd. Bet found her speaking with Emily and two other women, who had been trying to find something to eat for those who had stayed behind.

"How are you feeling, Mom?" Bet asked, placing a gentle hand on her mother's arm.

Margaret smiled at her, tired but resolute. "I'm fine, sweetheart. Now that things seem to have calmed down, there's much to do here to help the others."

Bet nodded, not too surprised by her mother's response. Margaret had always had that quiet strength, that desire to care for others before thinking of herself.

James was packing his things in the distance when he glanced at Bet, who returned his look, longing to join him. "Are you staying here? I'm going with James to check the situation in town," she said to her mother.

"Yes, Bet. I'll stay to help. The library has become a safe haven for many, and we need to get everything organized. Go ahead."

Bet embraced her tightly, letting herself be comforted for a moment by that maternal security that, despite everything, had never left her. "Be careful, Mom."

"Always," Margaret replied with a faint smile. "Go now. James is waiting for you."

Bet turned and found James near the door, his gaze fixed on her. The desire to be by his side was strong, and after one last goodbye to her mother, she walked toward him, ready to leave behind the horrors they had lived through.

The streets of Richmond were silent. The constant drone of cicadas that had tormented their minds seemed to have faded, leaving behind an almost surreal emptiness. Bet walked beside James, still incredulous that it was all over—or so it seemed. The air was thick with a mix of relief and melancholy as their footsteps echoed on the deserted sidewalk.

Bet stopped for a moment, taking a deep breath. The silence of the city, once oppressive, now had an almost peaceful quality. She looked at James beside her, his shirt dirty and dark circles under his eyes, clear signs of what they had been through. Yet, in that instant, she couldn't help but notice how different he seemed—more human, more vulnerable.

"How are you?" Bet asked, breaking the silence that had enveloped them since they left the library.

James looked at her, his eyes deep and full of emotion. "I'm... trying to understand," he replied with a half-smile. "I'm still dazed, but I think it's finally over."

"I hope so too," Bet murmured, her thoughts drifting between the relief of having survived and the weight of those they had lost along the way. "I can't believe we really stopped it. It feels like a dream."

James nodded, walking closer to her. She could feel the warmth of his body near hers, and the closeness gave him a sense of comfort he hadn't expected to find in such a situation. "You're not the only one who feels that way," he said, his voice a whisper between them. "Every time I close my eyes, I still see those cicadas. That sound... and everything that happened. I can't get it out of my head."

Bet looked at him. "I know, I feel the same," she admitted, sensing a strange connection between them at that moment. It was as if all the emotions —the fear, the anguish—had finally found a release. They had spent so much time fighting, just trying to survive, that now, with this sudden peace, they didn't know what to do.

They walked on for a few more minutes until James suddenly stopped, pointing to a side street. "My house is that way," he said, his voice calmer. "I'd like to check if everything's okay. You can come with me if you want."

Bet stared at him, her heart beating hard in her chest. There wasn't just the echo of fear and pain, but something else—something deeper that had grown between them. It had been there the whole time, hidden beneath the surface of their interactions, but now it was impossible to ignore. Bet felt the desire to be with him, to not let him go. Not anymore.

A trembling smile tried to hide the emotion overwhelming her, her eyes fixed on him. "Of course, I'll come with you."

They resumed walking side by side, each step drawing them closer, not just physically but emotionally too. Bet felt excitement growing inside her, a desire that went beyond the simple need for companionship. She wanted to be near

James, to share everything they had been through, without any more barriers. Her mind filled with memories: the sleepless nights, the silent battles against the sound that had threatened to annihilate them. All of it had nurtured something different, something that was now emerging with an irresistible force.

They arrived at James's house, a small dwelling tucked among the trees, which Bet already knew. The porch light was dim, but bright enough to make James's eyes shine as he turned to her. "I haven't had time to clean up," he said with a nervous laugh, "but you know the place."

Bet shook her head, smiling. "Don't worry, James. Your home represents you, and I like it."

They entered in silence, closing the door behind them as if they wanted to shut out the rest of the world. The inside of the house was simple, but cozy. Bet felt immediately at ease, as if this place had always been a refuge for her.

James moved toward the kitchen, turning on a small lamp that cast a warm glow in the room. "Want something to drink?" he asked, but his

voice held a slight tension, as if he already knew that wasn't the real question.

Bet shook her head, her eyes never leaving James's. "No," she answered softly. "I'm not thirsty."

For a moment, there was only silence between them. Then, almost without thinking, Bet moved closer to him, feeling the air thick with something much stronger than either of them. Their bodies were just inches apart, and Bet could feel the warmth of James's breath on her face. Her heart pounded, no longer from fear, but from the intensity of the moment.

"James..." she murmured, but the words faded as he gently took her by the waist, pulling her toward him. There was no need for explanations, no words. Their desire, suppressed until then, finally found its release.

Their lips met softly, a shiver of desire passing between them, making them forget, if only for a moment, everything they had been through. James's hands moved tenderly along Bet's body, as if he wanted to savor every inch of her. And she responded with equal intensity, holding onto him as if he were the only thing keeping her grounded in that reality.

Their breaths grew more intense, blending together in a frantic yet sweet rhythm. When James lifted her slightly and carried her toward the sofa, Bet didn't resist. She let herself fall into his arms, feeling the warmth of his body surrounding her completely. In that moment, everything felt right.

Every movement was a celebration of their love, their survival. He gently unbuttoned her shirt and took off his sweat-soaked one. James's hands moved delicately along Bet's back, making her tremble, while she clung to him, trying to forget all the pain. Every touch was a promise, every kiss a way to banish fear. They were alone, in their world, and nothing outside of them existed.

When they finally let go completely, their love exploded into a passion that was both sweet and desperate. Their bodies moved together as if they had always been meant to complete each other. Bet felt every emotion wash over her: pain, joy, love—

all mixed in a single wave of sensations that made her cry with gratitude.

Bet's tears mingled with James's kisses, as he held her even tighter, as if afraid of losing her. "Don't ever leave," he whispered, his voice broken with emotion. "We're meant to be together."

Bet looked into his eyes, her face streaked with tears but with a smile that spoke of hope. "I'm not going anywhere. I've always belonged to you," she replied, as her lips softly brushed against his.

Their bodies fused, making love as if it were the last thing they would ever do, as if every kiss, every touch, was a prayer for the future they had feared they would never have. Their hearts beat as one, and every spasm, every movement, was a celebration of their love, in the throes of an explosion of desire.

They stayed entwined on the sofa, the world seeming to have returned to its place. The pain, the suffering, everything they had been through was still there, but now it seemed easier to face. Together.

James's fingers slowly traced the line of Bet's back, and she, breathing deeply, closed her eyes, savoring the feeling of peace she hadn't felt in a long time.

The silence that enveloped them was different from the one they had known in recent days. It wasn't the menacing silence, thick with incessant chirping and suffocating anxiety. It was a peaceful, intimate silence that allowed them to breathe and feel each other in a way they never thought possible.

Bet lay nestled in James's arms, his warmth against her own, his skin like a protective blanket shielding her from everything they had endured. She clung to him as if to absorb his strength, but no matter how safe she felt, the memories wouldn't fully disappear. The images of Sarah at the church, Mrs. Anderson and her grandson, the devastation in Richmond—they resurfaced in her mind like ghosts refusing to leave. Yet, in that moment, wrapped in James's embrace, Bet felt a profound sense of protection. For the first time in a long while, she didn't have to fight alone.

Slowly, she lifted her gaze and saw James watching her. There was something new in his eyes, a light she hadn't noticed before. Perhaps it was gratitude for surviving, or perhaps something deeper—something that had taken root over the time they had spent together, fighting against something that could have broken them. But it hadn't. They were here, together, and that was all that mattered.

"I've always wanted to tell you something," James began, his voice low and heavy with emotion. "But I could never find the right moment."

Bet looked at him intently, her heart beating faster. "What is it?" she asked, her voice barely a whisper.

James took a deep breath, as if gathering courage. "Ever since you came back to Richmond, I've realized that... there's always been something between us, Bet. Even when we were younger. But now, after everything we've been through, I don't want to ignore it anymore."

His words hit her deeply. Bet realized that she, too, had always felt that connection, that bond. It had been easy to overlook it when life had separated them, but now there was no more doubt. They were meant to be together.

Bet rested her forehead against James's, feeling the warmth of his breath mingling with her own. "Me too," she said, her words full of truth. "I've always known."

For a moment, they stayed like that, just breathing together, letting the world pause around them. The weight of their fears and pain slowly dissolved, replaced by an infinite sweetness that wrapped around them like a cocoon. It was as if they had finally found a safe harbor, a place where they could let go without the fear of being broken again.

"I love you, Bet. I always have," James whispered, breaking the silence with words that vibrated with sincerity.

Tears filled Bet's eyes, but this time they weren't tears of pain or fear. They were tears of relief, of joy. She kissed him gently, letting her lips convey everything she couldn't put into words. "I love you too..." she whispered back, her voice nearly choking on the happiness flooding her.

James held her even tighter, as if making sure she would never slip away. "I'm never letting you go," he said, his voice firm and resolute.

"Don't," Bet replied, knowing that those words were a promise he would keep.

For the first time in what felt like forever, Bet felt truly free. Their love, born and strengthened from the ashes of suffering, was a beacon that would light the way to their future. They fell asleep like that, wrapped around each other, with the knowledge that, despite everything, the worst was behind them.

And together, they would face whatever came next.

The morning light filtered through the trees, casting soft shadows across the room. Bet stirred, the warmth of James's body still next to hers, comforting and reassuring. For a moment, she allowed herself to bask in the calm, in the serenity of knowing that they had survived, that they had each other.

But soon, reality would come knocking.

Bet slowly disentangled herself from James's embrace and slipped out of bed. As she dressed, memories of the past days returned to her with force. The people they had lost, the battle they had fought—none of it would simply disappear because they had found peace in each other. There was still much to rebuild, wounds that would take time to heal.

James woke as Bet was pulling on her boots, his eyes slowly adjusting to the daylight. "You're up early," he mumbled, his voice groggy with sleep.

Bet smiled softly, walking over to the bed to kiss him on the forehead. "There's a lot we need to do," she said quietly. "Richmond isn't going to fix itself."

James stretched, sighing as the weight of responsibility settled in once more. "You're right. But for a little while longer, I just want to stay here with you."

Bet's heart warmed at his words, but she knew they couldn't stay hidden in this cocoon forever.

"We'll have more moments like this," she promised. "But for now, people need us."

He nodded, sitting up and running a hand through his messy hair. "Let's see what's left of the town, then."

Together, they left the house, stepping back into the world that had almost destroyed them. The streets of Richmond were still eerily quiet, but in the distance, Bet could hear faint signs of life—people beginning to emerge from the ruins, determined to rebuild.

As they walked, James took Bet's hand in his. They didn't speak much, but the silence between them was no longer heavy. It was filled with understanding, with a bond that went deeper than words. Whatever came next, they would face it side by side.

When they reached the center of town, they found Margaret already hard at work, organizing groups of survivors, offering comfort to those who needed it. She looked up when she saw them approach and smiled, a tired but hopeful expression on her face.

"Good, you're here," Margaret said, her voice filled with quiet determination. "We've got a lot of work to do."

Bet exchanged a glance with James, and he squeezed her hand gently. "Let's get to it," she said, feeling stronger than she had in days.

As the three of them began working together to rebuild what had been lost, Bet couldn't help but feel that despite the pain, despite the scars they would all carry, something new was growing in Richmond. A future that was theirs to shape, one step at a time.

And for the first time in a long while, Bet felt hope. Real, tangible hope.

Together, they would rebuild, not just the town, but their lives. And no matter what shadows still lurked at the edges of their memories, they knew they had each other.

And that was enough.

Chapter 16: The Shadow of Sound

Time seemed to have finally granted Richmond a reprieve. The quiet that enveloped the city was a reflection of a hard-won peace, like a deep breath after teetering on the edge of the abyss. Bet and James had traversed the darkness together, and now, with the future ahead of them, everything seemed brighter.

Seven months had passed since that nightmare, and Bet's belly had grown noticeably larger. She was expecting a child with James—a tangible sign of life, hope, and rebirth. Every day, as she caressed her steadily rounding belly, she felt the future pulsing inside her.

Bet's mother, Margaret, had started treatments for her illness and was showing slight improvement. Emily and Walker regularly met in the library, working on their research and spending time together after the dramatic events they had all endured. The survivors had returned to their daily lives, but despite the regained silence, an unnatural calm lingered over Richmond. The people were still marked by the nightmare they had lived through.

That afternoon, the sun shone high in the sky, but it seemed pale, almost distant. The air was still, as if even the wind had stopped, holding its breath. Everything was too quiet. The laughter, the voices that once filled the streets of the city, seemed like distant, almost unreal memories.

In recent weeks, Bet had noticed something strange. James had changed. His restlessness had become palpable, like a shadow that quietly draped over him. He spent hours in his study with the door closed, still working on that cursed record. He told her he just wanted to be sure—sure that it was really over, sure there were no more traces of that sound, sure their child could grow up happy and safe. But Bet, deep down, knew there was something more. Every time she saw him get out of bed in the middle of the night, his gaze vacant and his movements stiff, she understood that something was wrong.

While they were having dinner that evening, Bet noticed something different in James's eyes. "Is everything okay?" she asked.

James only nodded, kissed her growing belly, and retreated to bed. "I'm just really tired, I'm going to sleep," he said, rising from the table with a strange expression.

After cleaning up in the kitchen, Bet joined him in bed, but she fell asleep with an uneasy feeling. A few hours later, she woke up with a start, a shiver running down her spine. She turned her head to the side of the bed where James should have been, but his spot was empty, the covers cold and abandoned. The room was silent, but not in a comforting way. That silence weighed heavily on her, like a foreboding presence she couldn't shake.

Bet sat up, but her body felt heavier than usual, her swollen belly a constant reminder of how much her body had changed. Every movement was accompanied by a slight discomfort, a weight that made her feel clumsy and slow. She rose slowly, trying not to make too much noise, but her heart began to pound harder in her chest. "James?" she called, but there was no response.

She walked through the hallway, passing the kitchen and living room, but James wasn't there. The darkness of the house made her feel even more isolated. Her breathing grew shallow, her breath catching in her throat as she advanced, her swollen belly giving her a feeling of instability. She clung to the wall to keep her balance. Each step felt like a struggle, as if something wanted to hold her back, to prevent her from reaching James's study.

The door to his study was ajar, a faint light leaking through the crack. Bet approached, her breath shallow and her hands trembling. A growing emptiness inside her warned her of what she was about to find on the other side of the door. Sleep had become impossible for him. Something dark had him in its grip. She placed her hand on the door handle and, with the slightest push, stepped inside.

James was sitting at his desk, headphones on. His eyes were fixed in a blank stare, his hands limp at his sides. There was something wrong with his face, an absence that made Bet's blood run cold. His shoulders were stiff, his muscles taut like cords ready to snap.

"James..." Bet whispered, moving slowly toward him.

There was no reaction. His breathing was steady, but there was an unnatural stillness in his body, as if he were trapped in a state of suspension between life and death.

"James!" she shouted louder, shaking him by the shoulders. Still nothing. Bet's heart raced, a terror paralyzing her mind as it started to take over.

With trembling hands, she reached up and removed the headphones from his head. Blood trickled from his ears, staining the collar of his pajamas, and Bet was struck by a faint but chilling sound: the chirping of cicadas. That cursed sound was still there, alive in the headphones, an invisible presence that had never truly left them. Bet held her breath. It was as if the sound had returned, like a ghost slipping between them, stealing James's soul.

James didn't move. His face was blank, completely devoid of emotion. His mind... was gone.

"James, what have you done?" Bet screamed, gripping the headphones in a fury, throwing them to the ground as if they were the source of all the evil. The sound abruptly stopped, but the echo of the chirping still seemed to resonate within the walls of the room. Her hands trembled as she stared at James's body—her man, her love— completely absent. "James, answer me! Please, answer me!" she cried desperately, shaking his shoulders, but his gaze remained vacant, unresponsive. There was nothing left to do.

Tears began to fill her eyes, blurred by despair as she collapsed in front of him, taking his face in her hands. "James! Please, answer me!" Her voice broke, a scream choked by pain, by the hollow emptiness that was devouring her from the inside. James's body was still there, but his soul, his mind... had been sucked into a darkness from which he would never return. Bet knew it, and the thought tore her heart apart.

Clutching James's face to her chest, Bet whispered desperate prayers, as if her words could bring him back, as if she could still save him. "You can't leave me. Not like this. Not now…" But James didn't respond. His eyes were lost in a void Bet couldn't bear to face.

The room was heavy with silence, but in Bet's mind, the chirping of cicadas still echoed, a refrain of despair that wouldn't stop. She was alone. Completely alone.

With a scream of anguish, Bet let go of James's head and collapsed to the floor. She couldn't believe what she had just seen. That nightmare, that sound, that record, the cicadas—they had haunted her life, ripping away first her father and now James.

She struggled to stand, dragging herself to the door of the study. Her legs trembled under the weight of her body and the baby she carried. Every movement felt clumsy, heavy, and the pain in her heart made everything even harder. She had to get out, she had to breathe, but when she flung open the front door to the driveway, she was met with an even more terrifying sight.

Richmond, the city she had believed saved, had returned to being a nightmare.

The people who had survived the horror months earlier now wandered the streets like shadows. Their movements were slow, mechanical. Their faces were twisted with empty, absent expressions, like James's. Some had blood streaming from their ears, others stared blankly into space with glassy, lifeless eyes. It was as if the city had been sucked back into a nightmare, but this time, there was no one to save them.

Bet stepped back, paralyzed by fear. The chirping of cicadas mixed with the low moans of the people wandering aimlessly, like lost souls in a land they no longer recognized. The figures outside seemed to belong to a different world, a distorted reality where the sound had taken control of their minds.

She recognized some of those people. There was Mrs. Dawson, the elderly neighbor who always smiled kindly when they met in the street. Now she staggered, her face contorted in an expression of silent terror. Mr. Cartwright, the mechanic who had fixed their car countless times, was slumped on the sidewalk, his bloody hands covering his ears as if desperately trying to block out that infernal sound.

Her heart pounded in her chest, her sweaty hands shaking. The sight overwhelmed her, and with a cry of horror, she slammed the door shut, barricading herself inside the house. Her breath caught in her throat, her heart beating so hard it felt like it would explode. Panic mounted within her, growing like a wave that suffocated her. She was alone. Completely alone.

Sharp pains suddenly gripped her belly, as if something inside her was twisting. "My baby…" she gasped, clutching her belly with trembling hands. "I have to stay calm. I have to sit down," she told herself. She fled to the living room, her body shaking as she curled up on the couch. There was no escape. She didn't know what to do. Her hands rested on her belly as if trying to protect the life she carried, but even that seemed in danger. Who would protect their baby now that James was gone and everything was falling apart?

The thought of the child inside her filled her with an even deeper anguish. The only remaining link to James, to the man she had loved, was that life pulsing within her. But how could she protect it, now that the world around them was crumbling? She reached for the phone to try to call her mother, but the line rang empty. No answer.

With tears streaming down her face, she turned on the television, desperately searching for an explanation, a sign that everything would be okay. But what she saw took her breath away.

On every channel, from every corner of the world, came reports of the same horror she was living. A sound, described as a hypnotic frequency, was driving people mad. The news showed images of devastated cities, of people wandering without consciousness, just like those she had seen outside the door. Every station repeated the same warning: "Barricade yourselves inside. Protect your ears. Don't listen to the sound."

Bet stared at the screen, her eyes brimming with tears, the world collapsing around her. That sound hadn't been stopped, not completely. And now, it had claimed everything: her city, the man she loved, and maybe even their future.

She fell back onto the couch, her breathing labored. Every fiber of her body seemed to give way under the weight of terror and despair. Her hands, once so strong, rested weakly on her belly, seeking reassurance that she knew was futile. The baby moved still, a small spasm of life, the only sign that something pure still existed in this shattered world.

But the chirping of the cicadas showed no sign of fading. It grew louder in her ears, as if each vibration of the sound was burrowing under her skin, penetrating her bones. The house, once a safe haven, now seemed to vibrate in unison with that cursed sound. The walls, the floors, every object around her seemed to be part of a great symphony of madness, orchestrated by an invisible force.

The sound buzzed incessantly in her ears, and every attempt to block it out was futile. Bet closed her eyes, hoping the darkness might offer her some peace, but all she found was a suffocating void, a space where the chirping only intensified.

The pain she felt for the loss of James mingled now with something deeper, more visceral. It was as if something inside her was changing, as if her very will was slowly slipping away, drained by the sound surrounding her. The tears still streamed down her face, but her hands moved automatically to wipe them away, as if her body was acting without her control.

The sound… It was all that remained.

Her gaze, once darting anxiously, became more and more fixed. Her eyes, which just minutes before had shone with terror and despair, began to lose their color. The deep blue of her irises faded, like a light slowly dimming. Her eyelids felt heavy, but she didn't close them. She couldn't move anymore. The exhaustion she felt was profound—not just physical, but mental—an utter depletion of all her strength.

Her hands, which had nervously clutched her belly, were now motionless. The chirping of the cicadas was the only thing she could hear, the rest of the world had vanished. The news on the television continued to broadcast images of destruction, of people driven mad, but Bet no longer saw them. Her gaze was fixed on the screen, but she wasn't really watching. The sound was everywhere— inside her, in her head, in her heart. Every thought was dissolving, swallowed by that incessant noise.

Her lips, once full of desperate words, relaxed into a thin line. Even the pain for James, for the future that would never be, began to fade, as if it was being slowly drained away by the void that the sound was creating within her.

Bet suddenly found herself motionless, unable to fight anymore. She could still feel the baby moving, but that movement, once a source of hope, was now just a distant echo, something she could no longer touch. Her breathing grew slower, more shallow. The beat of her heart seemed to align with the hypnotic rhythm of the cicadas.

And then it happened.

Her eyes dimmed completely, becoming two dark, empty wells. Her pupils dilated, unmoving, like those of the people she had seen outside James's house. Her face, once full of emotion, transformed into an expressionless mask. The tears stopped flowing, and her body, which had trembled with anguish moments before, relaxed completely.

The sound had won.

Bet remained there, sitting on the couch, unmoving, her gaze fixed on nothing. The chirping of the cicadas filled the house, bouncing off the walls, enveloping everything—every thought, every hope. There was no more fear, no more pain, no more hope. Only the sound.

Bet's face no longer changed. Her eyes, once so alive, were now lost, extinguished. And as the sound continued to echo, Bet had surrendered. Richmond had fallen. Bet had fallen too.

And the chirping of the cicadas, constant and unrelenting, continued to resonate, like the final requiem for a world that would never be the same again.

Richmond, their world, would never be the same again.

Chapter 17: The Revelation

Bet could no longer feel anything. The cicadas' chirping, which had filled her mind moments earlier, seemed to dissolve into an oppressive silence, a void slowly swallowing her. It was as if she were slipping into a dark, infinite abyss, a place where there was no room for sound, light, or time. Every breath grew fainter, blurred, like a distant memory as the darkness enveloped her completely.

Just when everything seemed lost, the door to the house burst open with a sudden crash, shattering the deadly silence. A beam of light cut through the dimness, tearing Bet from the stupor in which she had been sinking. In the doorway stood two figures, indistinct at first but slowly taking shape. It was Professor Walker and Emily. Both wore protective headphones, and even in her semi-conscious state, Bet recognized them.

Her foggy mind struggled to grasp something—a fragment of awareness that could anchor her to reality. But everything felt so distant, so unreachable.

Walker wasted no time. Without saying a word, he strode through the house with determined steps, ignoring the pain tightening around his heart. He headed straight for the study, already knowing what he would find. His hands trembled slightly as he approached the door, his heart heavy with apprehension and fear. And there, as he feared, was James. He was seated at the desk, motionless, his eyes vacant. His face was expressionless, and blood trickled from his ears—a clear sign that the cursed sound had claimed him too. The vinyl, the damned record, still spun on the turntable, a relic of destruction that had already claimed too many victims.

"James..." Walker whispered, his voice breaking with grief. He felt a tightness in his chest, a pain that paralyzed him. He approached slowly, as if his mind refused to comprehend what he was seeing. Though he knew there was nothing more to be done, he gently shook James, desperately hoping for a reaction, a sign of life. But James's body remained inert, a hollow shell, devoid of soul. The

sound had destroyed his mind, leaving behind an unbearable emptiness.

Fighting back the tears that threatened to overwhelm him, Walker backed away from the lifeless body. The loss of his friend hit him with devastating force. But he couldn't allow himself to fall apart. There was no time for grief. Bet and the baby still had a chance. He had to act quickly; he had to protect them.

With a determined gesture, he wiped his eyes, trying to suppress the pain. His gaze fell on the turntable, where the vinyl continued to spin slowly in silence. The record was the source of it all, and Walker knew he couldn't leave it behind. He grabbed it with sudden anger, stuffed it into the bag he had brought, and left the room without looking back. Leaving James like that tore at his heart, but he had to think of Bet. There was no other choice.

When he returned to the main room, he found Emily still kneeling beside Bet. Emily's face was pale, marked by anxiety and concern. The protective headphones were already secured over

Bet's ears, but something about her expression troubled Emily deeply. Her eyes were fixed on Bet's rounded belly, and a deep unease radiated from her gaze.

"We can't leave her like this," Emily whispered, her voice breaking with anguish. "The baby... the sound could still reach him."

Walker looked at her, the realization hitting him like a punch. The baby, defenseless in the mother's womb, could be exposed to that cursed sound despite Bet's headphones. The cicadas' chirping was an invisible enemy, capable of penetrating everywhere, seeping into minds and bones, destroying everything.

"What can we do?" Walker asked, frustration and panic creeping into his voice. They didn't have much time.

Emily was silent for a few seconds, her brain racing to find a solution. Then an idea began to form. Without a word, she stood and ran to the bedroom. She returned moments later with a pile of heavy blankets in her arms. "If the headphones aren't enough to protect the baby, we have to try to insulate the sound another way. We need to wrap her belly in these blankets. It's not a perfect solution, but it might dampen the sound enough to keep the baby safe."

Walker nodded, realizing they had no better options. He grabbed one of the blankets, and together with Emily, began wrapping it around Bet's belly. Each layer of fabric seemed like a desperate attempt to create a barrier against the invisible threat surrounding them. Walker's hands shook slightly as he worked quickly, fully aware that time was running out. The cursed sound could overwhelm them at any moment.

The cicadas' chirping continued to grow in intensity, filling the air with a vibration that seemed to resonate in their bones. The windows rattled slightly, as if the sound was trying to force its way into the house, into their minds. Walker's heart pounded in his chest, his breath short and labored, leaving no room for coherent thought. They had to hurry.

"Walker…" Emily murmured, her face tight with tension. "We can't leave her here. We need to get her out of here now."

"Yes," he replied, his voice grim. "Let's get her to our van. The library is the only safe place left."

Together, they managed to lift Bet. Her body felt heavier than usual, weighed down by the child she carried and the blankets that now swaddled her. But the strain didn't matter. Every step they took was laden with tension, every movement seemed slowed by the growing terror that the chirping could overtake them at any moment.

Once outside, they swiftly loaded Bet into the back of the van. Emily made sure she was settled carefully, ensuring the blankets remained securely wrapped around her belly and the headphones firmly in place over her ears. They couldn't afford any mistakes. There was no room for failure.

Walker climbed into the driver's seat, his heart pounding so loudly it echoed in his ears. The engine roared to life, and the van sped off, leaving behind James's house and its dark fate.

As they drove through the deserted streets of Richmond, the cicadas' chirping seemed to chase them, an invisible wave enveloping them, seeping into every crevice of the air. It was as if the sound was aware of their attempt to escape and was pursuing them with all its fury. The streets of the city were now ghostly, the houses abandoned, and the few remaining humans wandered like mindless shadows, their faces twisted by madness. The bloody ears of those people were the last sign of what they had been before the sound consumed them.

Emily stared at Walker with fear-filled eyes, unable to stop the tears streaming down her pale face. Just hours ago, everything had seemed normal—at least as normal as it could be in a city that had seen days of terror. And now everything was falling apart. "Walker... what's happening? Why now?" she asked in a trembling voice. "How did we get to this point?"

He pressed his lips together, his eyes fixed on the road ahead. His hands gripped the steering wheel so tightly that sweat gathered under his palms. How could he answer that question? How could he tell Emily that he and James had known for some time that the city wasn't safe? He would lose her trust, but he had no choice. He couldn't hide the truth any longer. "Emily," he admitted, his voice filled with regret, "when we connected the device to the monolith... one of the cables attached to the monolith came loose because of the strong vibration in the cave. We thought we destroyed the sound of the cicadas, but we didn't realize the frequency of the ritual, the one that was supposed to silence the sound permanently, didn't complete its process. Everything was set up—the frequencies, the recording, and the two cables—but we failed."

Emily stared at him in disbelief, unable to accept what she was hearing. "But... we thought we stopped it..."

Walker shook his head. "Not completely," he said gravely. "We thought we had solved everything, but we didn't have time to fully understand it. Maybe it all started again. I don't know, but now the sound is spreading, not just here, but everywhere, to all the cities in the world. James and I were trying to figure out how to stop it, but..." his voice broke, remembering the scene he had just witnessed.

The silence that followed was even more chilling. The deserted streets of Richmond seemed to scream in their eerie quiet, while the cicadas' chirping roared invisibly, destroying everything.

At last, they arrived at the library, their only remaining hope. The large stone structure stood like a fortress against the chaos raging outside. Walker parked quickly, and together with Emily, he lifted Bet from the back of the van, carrying her inside. The heavy doors of the library closed behind them with a resounding thud that echoed through the silence, as if sealing the despair outside, at least for now.

The library was bathed in an unnatural calm, as if it existed in another world compared to the one outside. The thick walls, built to stop and absorb that dark sound, still held strong, but they wouldn't last forever.

As soon as they entered the main hall, a figure moved in the shadows. It was Margaret, Bet's mother. Emily and Walker had brought her there earlier, when the sound had started spreading through the city again. Margaret had waited with her heart full of anguish, praying that her daughter was still alive. And now, her prayer had been answered—but at a devastating price.

When she saw Bet lying on the couch in the main hall, Margaret's breath caught in her throat. Her daughter, her only daughter, looked so fragile, so distant. She was wrapped in blankets, a cocoon that separated her from the outside world but couldn't shield her from the pain Margaret felt. Without saying a word, she rushed to her side, tears silently streaming down her face. Every step was a battle against the horror she felt.

She knelt beside Bet, her trembling hands caressing her pale face. "Bet…" she whispered, her voice utterly broken by despair. Her daughter couldn't be reduced to this, not after everything they had done, not after saving the city, not after carrying the life growing inside her. With a gentle gesture, Margaret placed her hands on Bet's belly. Beneath the blankets lay a life, fragile and precious. The baby had to survive. It was the only hope left in a world that was falling apart.

Margaret leaned down, resting her head against Bet's, as if the mere touch could bring her back from the abyss into which she was slipping. "I won't leave you, my love. Not like this... I will protect you. I will try to protect you and your baby, no matter the cost."

As Margaret stroked Bet's belly, she felt a slight movement. The baby was still alive. It was weak, but it was a sign. A small glimmer of hope in an ocean of despair. Margaret held her breath, clinging to that fragile spark. It wasn't over yet.

Emily, watching the scene, couldn't hold back her tears. Even Walker, standing by the window trying to figure out how to end this nightmare, was overwhelmed by the pain Margaret felt. There was nothing more devastating than watching a mother fight for her daughter's life.

Margaret turned to Walker, her eyes filled with desperation. "Walker... please... we can't give up. You'll find a way, won't you? There has to be a solution... for Bet, for the baby."

Walker nodded, his gaze resolute. He couldn't find the right words. The fight wasn't over yet, but his mind felt clouded. Sighing deeply, he continued to stare out the window at the city, which was slowly dying before his eyes.

The sound, that cursed chirping, continued to coil outside the library, ready to claim everything, ready to destroy the last remaining hope.

Biography of Emmanuele Landini

Emmanuele Landini (born in 1975) is an Italian sound engineer, record producer, and creative professional with over 5,000 tracks to his name, created both for himself and for other artists and companies. From a young age, he developed a deep connection with sound and music, specializing in genres such as ambient, new age, and electro/ambient, distinguished by their unique and refined soundscapes.

In addition to his role as a sound engineer, Emmanuele stands out for his ability to craft innovative and sophisticated sound environments designed to fully enhance the artist and their music. His artistic sensitivity and extensive experience allow him to build sound landscapes that bring out the unique characteristics of each project, making a significant contribution to the success of the productions he is involved in.

A passionate researcher in the field of 3D binaural music, Emmanuele has dedicated part of his career to studying frequencies and biofrequencies and how they interact with the human body. This interest led to the publication of his book *"Il suono della follia"* *("The Sound of Madness")*, in which he explores the effects of sound vibrations on people's psychophysical states. The frequencies used in the book are grounded in scientific reality, reflecting his commitment to musical research and innovation.

Alongside his musical work, Emmanuele also has a deep passion for cinema, particularly the thriller and horror genres. This interest represents for him a kind of inner contrast and search present in every person. Drawn to dark atmospheres and gripping plots, he combines sound and visuals in innovative ways, creating immersive experiences that keep audiences on the edge of their seats.

An ever-evolving artist, Emmanuele Landini is constantly seeking new ways to express his talent. Each of his creations, whether auditory or narrative, offers insight into his vision of the world, inviting the audience on an emotional journey through sound, words, and images.

For more information about his works and projects, visit his website at emmanuelelandini.com.

www.spheredistribution.co.uk

Milton Keynes UK
Ingram Content Group UK Ltd.
UKHW032316121024
449481UK00011B/339